A SUNDAY IN HELL

With a new foreword,
Report From an Empty Grave,
and afterword by
Hugh MacDonald

Cody,

Being Sealed
with the Gifts of
the Holy Spirit, gives
you moral Authority to
be witness to the Truth
and a voice of change
in the world... Go
out there and Question
Authority on all levels
in this world we live
in... Be a voice for
the voiceless

Congratulations on making
Your Confirmation !!!

~Your Brother
in Christ,

Bob

Daniel Berrigan

A SUNDAY IN HELL

FABLES & POEMS

Daniel Berrigan

With an Afterword by Hugh MacDonald

B&B

Bunim & Bannigan
New York • Charlottetown

Published by BUNIM & BANNIGAN, LTD.
30 Jericho Executive Plaza, Suite 500W, Jericho, NY 11753
Box 636 Charlottetown, PEI C1A 7L3 Canada

www.bunimandbannigan.com

Manufactured in the United States of America

Design by Jean Carbain
Illustration: P. John Burden
Author Photo: John Toolan
2nd edition make-up: Matthew MacKay

Berrigan, Daniel.
A Sunday in hell : fables & poems / Daniel Berrigan;
with a new foreword by Daniel Berrigan;
with an afterword by Hugh MacDonald.
2nd edition, 2014

Library of Congress Control Number 2005035165

Library binding
ISBN 13: 978-1-933480-02

Trade paperback
ISBN 13: 978-1-933480-03-9

e-book
ISBN 1-933480-35-1
ISBN 978-1-933480-35-0

Second edition 2014

Heartfelt thanks to my editor Paul Williams,
who oversaw this unlikely project with verve and skill.

CONTENTS

As though
there were future,
as though
there were God.
Two premises
one; predicament, outcome.
This God I never see
until I forget to look
walking the waves, beckoning.
Until I learn to forget
the unbridgeable void between
that One and me—
I a land creature
can have no hope.

—from *Block Island*

To Philip

I marvel
how tears signify.
Literate at last,
I read
Through a glass darkly,
the rest.

Prologue:
Report from the Empty Grave[1]

This year I am celebrating a totally unexpected event. I have survived in the priesthood for thirty years, and for forty-three years in the Jesuits. I have heard a retort in some quarters, that the Church and the Jesuits have also survived me. Indeed. In any case, it seemed a good time for some rather serious, playful and joyous stock-taking. Which, on reflection, came down to something of self- questioning like this: how are your symbols going, are you still trying to imagine the real world, are your eyes seeing, your ears hearing, your heart beating, and this in a world which is largely dysfunctional? In a culture which lies there, terminally ill but still kicking. In a world of the blind and poor and deaf and dumb. Or again, living as I do in New York, the question took this form, "Are you still alive in the urban morgue?"

I am, on the whole, happy to report a firm 'yes' to these questions. One way of showing myself that I am still alive and on the move is to reflect that I am still, after some 40 years of it, at the job and the joy of writing poetry. I also write prose in many forms and on many subjects. The poetry seems a greater index of vitality to me, closer to the

---

1 Originally published in THOUGHT, Vol. 57, No. 224 (March 1982) as *Anniversary Poems: Report From An Empty Grave.*

soul, a better kind of sensor to translate the edgy way life has been going. So I want to concentrate upon the poetry and a kind of running commentary. Through it, I have been able to seize on and elaborate a number of crazy events, as well as a number of sane ones. Everything from the notorious exile and law-breaking, underground, and prison in the 60's and 70's, through the laborious and burdensome bread and butter daily survival and routine, setbacks and moods, downers and uppers, that life shoves in all our faces, no matter who.

May I say before going further, that gratitude is a kind of mystifying and constant angel of mine. I am so grateful for everything. Grateful for 30 years of priest's work, for 43 years among Jesuits, for my parents and my family. And for these poems, which seem to me undeserved and even miraculous. Poems that are a kind of dark bulb of existence. A perennial root that, in spite of all, keeps coming up and up. And I don't mean this gratitude as a merely ceremonial salvo shot off on occasion. An expression of gratitude, like a perennial root pulled up at the end of summer, comes out with a load of dark earth attached. I don't know whether I would serve things best by cleaning the root off, or whether I should merely toss the root on the cellar floor with all the dirt and worms attached. All that dark uncertainty. All that is sinuous and seemly—, even when the bulb appears dead to the world.

I was thinking as I put these notes together, about the past year, that alone, and where it had taken me. Work in a cancer hospital in the city, to the Pentagon, on to court and jail once more. Bouncing around the country like a shuttle-cock, facing large numbers of people with my own uncomprehending and dazed eyes. Stealing like a con artist, those rare days when I can "get lost" in order to reclaim a lost article, namely my own soul. And meantime, with almost a Greek sense of harsh necessity, watching my country go down a foul drain of waste and want, of violence and anomie. And watching my church, a kind of death watch in many ways, a post-Vietnam post mortem. A wake, as the Irish used to call it, compounded of triviality, and soul-tripping, and nostalgia. Watching also my beloved Jesuit Order.

Toe-to-toe with the culture in so many ways; mending its cyclone fences, sporting its mod clothing, talking the language of psychology and corporate management and liberal politics.

I confess, of course, to being a part of all this. Who is not? I am guilty of much of it; but I am trying to be less guilty. I like and honor, in this regard, Paul's admonition, "Do not be conformed to this world." Even when I honor those great words only in the breach. I translate the words though, in my own way, "Try to be marginal as possible to all this madness." Thus I found my way this year to a terminal cancer hospital in New York; where I could not do much for anyone, but where I could clean floors and hold the hands of the dying and serve them food and drink (much more, really, than I can do for my dying country, for my church, for my order). Again I went to the Pentagon where the stench of death is so severe as to shrivel the soul. There I chained myself to the doors with some friends like a vertical corpse, and was dragged away like a horizontal one. So it goes.

I also write poetry, because this is a way.of submitting my anger to a strict discipline. I do not want to live in the world and not be angry; neither do I want to die just yet. Nor do I want my anger to burn useless like a waste flame from an oil stack. Wanting to live, nursing my flame, I write. It is a way of surviving. It tells you your soul is kicking, that it is your own. Indeed, that it is inalienable property, not to be trespassed on by the mad tinkers and triflers, whether of the pentagonal or the charismatic variety.

Believe me, I would like to be faithful. I remember in this regard, the blank stares I drew once in Ireland at a retreat, for saying to a company of sisters and priests that I had been searching for years for someone to be obedient to. That was a conservative statement, a profoundly traditional one, and so I meant it. For I am persuaded, in Simone Weil's phrase, that obedience is a need of the soul. That without this proper scope and corrected shape and admonitory word, we languish and inflate and grow foolish to ourselves.

Indeed, I reflect, what reason have I to trust myself or to walk in my own light? I have reason only to go in fear and trembling, a kind of vessel of darkness. Indeed, I have only to look within or around me to see the catastrophic result of Biblical disobedience, the loss of human measure and modesty. I saw my country grown blind beyond healing and violent beyond imagining, dumping an Armegeddon on a distant and inoffensive people, without reason, outside any rule of law. In such a mad time, I used to ask myself, was I to aid my country? And if the latter, to whom could I go with my anger, my conscience and my torment? Who would say to me: you must resist? Who would say: break the iniquitous law, it is a chain on all our limbs? Who would say: your direction is just, walk in it, and I will walk with you?

I hope that the 'no' of my brother, my family, and my friends to the war, and our continuing 'no' to the nuclear build-up, the arms treaty, the doomsday machines being planned and built—that this 'no' is uttered within a larger 'yes'. Paul says simply in his letters to the Christians of Corinth that Jesus is the great 'yes' of the Father. A 'yes' was uttered in the days of His humiliation; in the form of a bloody 'no' to the principalities of this world, to state and to Church. A 'no' which earned for Him the prompt verdict of capital punishment.

I would like to be found faithful on the day of the Lord, and I have a poem to offer on this theme. The poem, I think, should not require a lot of preliminary tutoring. It means to say something quite simple. Whenever a government, even a revolutionary one, gets established, I know I'm an outsider again. I would like to be the friend and advocate of every new kid on the block, especially those who get worked over by a neighborhood bully called Sam. But the speed with which the new kid hitches on to the methods .of the bully never ceases to appall me. I find that I have to hitch on to other ways, peoples, clues. So the poem turns from the international scene (a conventicle of bullies, if ever there was one) and lingers around an old man and his dying wife who used to run a store on my street in New York.

Fidelity

Coming up Broadway, a fruitless evening
reception at UN, the 'revolutionary ambassador'
resounding like a stale ash tray or like
the secretary of any state you mention & reflecting

sadly, the old game starts again
before the bloody flag is hoisted dry.
Life's an Orson Welles turn out of Graham Greene;
the train rushes into a tunnel, our hero in fatigues
saunters down the careening aisle
of the 3rd class carriage
expansive, macho
he disappears into mirrors

Minutes later he stands there in diplomat's stripes
stiff as a sword cane. He's hardened, molten to mirror.

alas, folks, freaks, minority spirits, we've lost again.
It rains on Broadway, tears of knowledge.
I look for a store to buy a pen to blacken and blear
on a page, tears or rain. I'll walk to 104th Street

where my old friend the picture framer
propped a photo of his dead wife in the window.

> Rain worsens
> knowledge goes under

He was inefficient and faithful
she. was propped in a wheel chair like a cauliflower
in a stall, months and months. Every hour or so

> he lit a cigarette
> put it to her lips.
> One day
> a crazy old black woman
> named by me, Crazy Horse
> came by
> leaned convivially over

the speechless mindless creature, yelled
'how are you dearie?' and kissed her like a luv.

I've long pondered fidelity. You can't know
even Gerald Ford that lethal dummox might be snatched
from mad comics by his cancerous wife. When the old woman
grew hopelessly ill, he closed the cramped
musty curiosity shop at 2 pm each day, took a taxi

     to Misericordia hospital
     sat there at bedside
     all evening. One day
     slight good news;
     'she ate something, they've

stopped the intravenous feeding.' A merciful interlude only;
she died that night in his arms. On this foul foot path
mule track, death mile, oblivion alley, bloody pass
Broadway, pith and paradigm of the world, cutting the
50 States of Amnesia like a poisoned pie; a swollen Styx
an Augean drain ditch

     a lotus blooms.

He looks up grey faced as I come in. 'she went peacefully
your green plant was by her bed.'
Leave it at that. Still, wishing I could summon
for myself, for my friends, someday

     for the world at large
     especially the self damned
     the hypocrites, the power brokers
     the 'revolutionary ambassadors'

     a bare whiff
     of that bloom

like hand laid on hand signifying a sacrament.

When I edged in sideways
past the morose dying
woman, her wheelchair
lodged like an embolism
in the body politic,
her skin wrapped like a rodent's
in a moth-eaten muff
I came
not off magical Broadway
into Ripoff Boutique
but where
springs have source

stream meeting stream signifying a sacrament.

To someone like myself the question of Jesus arises, of faith in Him. Looking back, I could never think when or whether I had been introduced to Him. Was there such a point? I doubt it. I take it that this was the genius of my parents and of their parents and so on back. We had put on Jesus with the flesh and bones of our race, taking him in with our mother's milk. There was no conscious point of time in which we met Him. He was consubstantial with us, in the clumsy old-fashioned phrase. How precious that was and is to me! Jesus a reality both majestic and immanent, a dweller in the bloodline as well as in the clouds of heaven.

But wait a minute, something intervened. It was not that easy. Since 1970, I have been underground and fleeing the law for some four months, in and out of jail repeatedly. The big cultural billboards are all out of countenance with me; those that puff the face of Jesus as well as that of Uncle Sam. I had written a book while underground. It came from reading John of the Cross; I called it THE DARK NIGHT OF RESISTANCE. And I still love it. I wrote that book to work out my sense that, while I had been gifted with the reality of Jesus, I had also been "had." At least "had" in a certain supposition about Him, which my fitful and nightmarish life had proven false if not absurd. The supposition went something like this: the reality of Jesus could be taken in, apart from the reality of the cross. I had to question this. Could I come to some vital sense of Christ without having my life literally blown apart? Could I merely tread the old track in the old cassock or indeed in the new mod chic duds and still hold to my heart anything but an illusion? It came to me that the question was really asking me to start over, to retrace my steps, organically. To go into reverse, to turn around. And something else struck me.

The millennial induction of Jesus into our worldliness, our armies, our fascism and violence and fear, had not only betrayed me, it had undone Him as well. Western history was not only hostile to me, it had set its face against Christ. Could Jesus know Himself as we dealt with Him? Could we know him anymore in such robes as had been thrust on him by the Constantinian arrangement, so often repeated; Christ of the battle grounds, Christ of the colonizers, Christ of the consumers, Christ of racism, Christ of Roman diplomacy, Christ of the White House masses and the Pentagon prayer rooms, Christ of tax exempt property, Christ of the army chaplains and executive prayer breakfasts? What had we done to him? Why, we had split his soul in a thousand fragments. He had as much need of recovery and rebirth as I.

Or this, at least, was my poetic conceit. That He and I together would step back and back and back and back into a kind of fetal darkness, reduced to an egg, to one cell even; and thereupon I would recover something of a saving ironies and oppositions, the ying and yang, the dialectic contentions in which alone the truth would exist and persist.

A new beginning, a making new. The poem that came from all this, as you will shortly see to your dismay, is a kind of nightmare. But in its light, which will indeed be dim, I would be willing to say the following in prose.

Given the Gods of most of us, Christ must be an argument against
God's existence.
Given the Christ of most of us, the real Christ must be dumb
as an unhatched egg.
Given the madleap of the Gerasene swine over the brink, the only
sane direction for humans is: get back!
Given the gnostic confabulations of the charismatics and Teilhardians,
some folk had better go slow.

To Christ Our Lord

To believe
you have to disbelieve
unstitching like love's sweet
cheat, the day's meticulous rainbow

But these, jackals
on the spoor of jackals
eat you like dead bees
for lust of the honeycomb
scatter you, death's parade.

Then priests wheel in like bears on unicycles
overtrained, underpaid
like motorized brooms they love debris
their vocation;
        bees' husks, taffeta remnants
confetti, all that's left
of the dead parade

O golden goose named Pharaoh
      they made you glorious
         only for their kitchen—
    for lust of that savory
      pâté **ROMANITA**

Roman goose
guardian of San Angelo
honking the devils off the sacred
precincts
we found you dead & scattered
for lust of a golden egg
no sooner born
than, closed, clouded like an eye

You brood there in the dark
like your own egg
you glimmer there in the dark like a
world ransoming pearl—

like a petrified tree
your heart of stone
your gospel a stone
you
an argument against God's existence

and the jackals chorus—
if he were not if he were not

Unto myself then! I step back back back

what is done is undone
what is believed is disbelieved

I whisper
like the first day of winter
disbelieve!
and close my eyes
like a wintry animal
and stop my heart in its shroud
and forbid life, and life giving metaphors.

On to my third poem. My sense of the Catholic Church is at base quite simple. I love it, and wish to live at peace in this communion. That is the basis I go from. The trouble is that neither my Church nor myself normally operate at base. Indeed, all of us step off base every morning of our lives to function in a Church and a world which are literally off their rockers. Off base. Off their base as well as ours. Worlds apart from us and our suppositions and visions. The Church in America moreover is desperately struggling to keep a remote resemblance to the community of Christ. More often than not, it loses rounds in this struggle; by default, by cop-out, by bargaining away the patrimony, by a thousand different oaths of induction into Caesar's bed and board.

I don't want to dwell on this. The plight of millions of American Catholics, I think, is roughly parallel to the plight of millions of other Americans. That is, we are decent, thoughtful, resilient, anxious to live in a way that is not coercive or death dealing. Still it cannot be denied that we decent people do many indecent things in the great world. That furious and desperate world is our judge. It cannot be denied we coerce and grab, instead of taking our rightful share, or sharing our rightful take. That the love of possessions is a sickness with us. That we form a vast support network for international sins of omission: omission of food, omission of housing, omission of dignity and a share of humanity.

Indeed, all of this could make a kind of spurious sense in America, if it brought a sense of well being or content even to our own people. We know it does not. In our case, the law of the universe rises up like a squad of Furies crying, "Too much is too little." Our war with the universe comes home. The nuclear nation nukes itself long before it announces Armageddon. What holds together today? Does marriage, or friendship, or public integrity or oaths of office or vows of religion? And above and beyond all this debris and regret and wrongheartedness, we have a leadership, political and religious (it is all pretty much the same) which ranges from the absolutely appalling to the downright dead.

What are we to do with our lives? The saving institutions are bankrupt. We have to start over in the church as well, picking over the bare bones of what has been reduced and rendered like the flesh of animals. It is a sorry business, it barely produces a living.

My poem, however, is playful as well as serious. I saw once in the transept window of Chartres Cathedral, four evangelists perched on the shoulders of four prophets. The conception was breathtaking and stark, a balancing act. The one below must take the weight of the future, the one above must see further, must tell what he sees, must use all that borrowed strength and height to deal a further prophetic word. Even as I reflected on it, it became a kind of circus act. As though the two, prophet and evangelist, stood there on a high wire, part of the great circus of creation that we call the Church. Where the actions are all death defying; Where animals and people are in concert and in conflict. Where freaks are on view. Where the drab routine of life in the world is relieved and refreshed and shaken up. Where indeed (this goes for the best circuses) no one does merely one thing. Where roles and costumes are interchanged, where all sorts of menial and skilled people do every skilled and menial thing, under the great central pole in the vast, airy tent.

There is another image in the poem. The old voyagers used to speak of sailing by the stars. It seems to have worked rather well. It required, of course, a detailed knowledge of those celestial skies, more accurate by far than the sketchy geography they had of the earth's surface. More to the point of a poem, the stars peopled the heavens with a company of glory; heroes and demi-gods and goddesses granted the earthbound an epiphany, stretched the human gaze up ward.

At least one of those stars stood firm, we are told, while the other creatures and creators danced about it. The North Star. I thought that very nice as fact and metaphor. The North Star gave point to the action above and direction to the action below, corresponding quite neatly to the double universe spoken of by the Greeks and borrowed by the author of the Letter to the Hebrews and the Book of Revelation. In any case, enough prose; here is the poem.

O Catholic Church

I would love you more if
  you would mother me less, if you
    egged on like a shrew by expensive shrinks
      and your own shrinking shadow
        weren't such an
      Amazon of Order

Sometimes I dream of you, a
  circus act; I'm performing
    under the tent's navel, swinging out
over and over, hundreds of feet up
    1/2 million eyes down there are peeled

  can't believe the act; and you're the
      anchor rope, the
     lynch pin, the
    center pole

        no; better, it's
        your act and mine!
our skills, our courage perfectly mutual
      tonight you're on my shoulders;
       the long horizontal pole vibrates with the subdued
     energy, passion, anguish of the world
North to south pole, everyone in touch with everyone
      horrendous, exultant news passing through the light grip
     of your hands and mine
      and we move
        and we move it
      and we are moved

Making one body vertical functional ecstatic—
     a figure of the future?
  a window of Chartres, evangelists on the shoulders of prophets
    two freedoms making a less imperfect freedom
      one held breath

impales two bodies, one heart beat
eyes on the twanging wire, hands
fused with the steel pole

Then sometimes I dream you're the north star.

And (this is no dream)
though I am forced to eat papier mâché for breakfast
and fret for the death of my friends
served up like cat and dog food
to alley cats, to mad dogs—
noble souls whose only offense is
they oppose the recycling of kangaroos into
the elegant eclair shit of
Park Avenue pimps
Still
if you are the north star you should say so now and then;
not incessantly,
not with a xerox blizzard from outer space
but with a word from a starry mouth
heard softly here and there, but with authority too

—a forefinger pointing
—a voice saying 'north'

We could infer the other directions;
south, east, west; and their
finer divisions, down to the hair lines

But not knowing north from south, our true direction
this is our madness!
And you could relieve it!

Pope John, from northern Italy, once helped.

The Ring

I wear my mother's wedding ring
who lack her voice, her smile.
Carol gave it in my hand
as a last gift, first really
and only relic, lonely
as we are. We are her post
mortem, altered. No, faith says
post vitam. I believe.
I kiss it like a bridegroom
and slip the narrow band on
which like her new existence has
no north south east west
but is like Saturn's ring, beyond
and like gold unmined, within.
If it were a sea shell I could
listen, but it rests there dumb.

One thought I have, who never
married. She wedded
and conceived me, and pushed me
away, into my own
eventual responsibility.
And then we buried her
close in nature, and I inherited
This golden pledge. I wish to be
as well myself, woman too
and lonely as I am
and scarce half what I would be
must borrow from the dead
and from little children, that
tenderness, awe, long loneliness
that are her planet's ring
of light, our unmined gold.

Daniel Berrigan, S.J., N.Y., NY 1982

A SUNDAY IN HELL

Lightning Struck Here

If stones can dream, after some hundred years
shouldering weight, making a wall inch onward
heaving it up a hill, braking its roll,
being only half above ground, taking the crack

of frost, the infernal sun, the insinuating, sleepy moss:—
if stones can long to stand up naked, a new creation
a horizon; where the wall goes
what shires, forests, it holds—
                              I suppose the dream
might rise, might arc, take color and stance of these
birches that fan out suddenly, bursting the wall
so when we come on them, all that remains
is a shambles. Lightning struck here
is a first thought. But no: a dream
shook from the mud, the interminable years, and lives

—from *Time Without Number*

The Hole in the Ground
A Parable for Peacemakers

There were once a people who were bored with winning. Winners! They were number one in everything: first in jogging, first in smoking, first in money making, and first in reality TV. They were first in per capita number of psychiatrists, spin doctors, lobbyists, morticians, and millionaires. You name it, they were it. They were first in war, first in peace, first in being first.

There was only one rub to this paradisiacal scene. People were bored.

"So we've done it again, big deal," they complained, switching off the tube. "Same old firsts: Olympics, consumers, smart bombs, gross national product."

They grew cynical, ungrateful to their national icons: the fitness celebrities, tycoons, news anchors, politicians, movie stars.

"First again, big deal. It's not that we're so hot, more like lousy competition." So it went.

Dangerous. They were on the way to another kind of record; first in national boredom. Their president was informed of the situation. Not exactly a strong and raging fire in these or other matters; still, always leisure time on his hands, he gathered his counselors.

Silence settled down. The president lathered himself into a fine virtuous contention, oozing with self-righteousness. "You're supposed to be advising me, keeping me on the ball? Well let's hear it; advise the heck out of me. Fact is, people are bored with our act. It possibly hasn't occurred to you," he fumed, "but a bored citizenry is dangerous, a national sitting duck, pickings for the axis of evil." He hit them high; he hit them low; mixing metaphors like mad. No boredom here.

Finally he stood up. "All right, meeting's over. And don't come back till you've thought up something unboring, some national project that'll get people off their royal American sitcom!"

He stormed out.

The advisers scattered, dejected. Some shrugged off the scolding, some were perplexed, and some plowed with worry. A few even gave attention into ways and means of unboring the USA.

This was hardly a frolic. More than a few of the president's men were themselves bored to desolation: with him, with themselves, with wheels and deals, wives, junkets, scrounging kids, suburbia. They fretted away; how the heck do you fish-line others out of the sludge when you're stuck in it yourself up to your follicles?

Another summons from the Oval Office.

And Eureka! One of the president's closest friends, a former exterminator from Texas, blew into Washington like a comet, eyes shooting inspiration like a struck oil well. The meeting reassembled. Our genius fastened himself to a seat at the right hand of power. It was clear from the word that got around that the President's mood hadn't improved, despite all that R and R at Camp David.

Undaunted, our Texan commenced in a thick Texas drawl: "Mister President, we've got it," he cried, not forgetting that old rah-rah plural. "Now hear this. How about if we dig the biggest, widest, deepest hole in the history of the world? Just think of it . . . give it a minute." He held up his hand, palm out. Restraint—slow down. "Think—give it time. Millions of bored citizenry put to useful labor, billions of stagnant dollars rollin' again." His arms made gigantic dollar signs in midair; saliva sprayed like a benediction on his American-flag lapel pin.

The president spontaneously combusted. They saw he was excited, the gleam leapt from eye to eye around the table. It was like ten Wall Streets about to go bullish. "Splendid!" boomed the president; and "Splendid!" went up and down, back and forth, a sonic boom and its echo.

"See it in your mind's eye, see it clear," shouted the exterminator statesman. "Biggest thing since the day o' creation!"

The president held up his hand, benignly, restraining. "We're on," he said solemnly. "But just remember, mum's the word. Why, what do you think you know who would be shortly up to (grammar was not his strong suit) if a leak went unplugged?"

The counselors leaned forward respectfully; they knew a rhetorical question when they heard one. "I'll tell you what they'd be up to," he went on fervently, "They'd snatch our blueprints, that's what they'd do. Or launch an attack. No sir, nothing leaves this room, not a word to your favorite white-walled grandmother—anyone."

So it was done. In a remote corner of the land, out of sight of TV snoops, moles, terrorists, creeps, the dig started.

The vast machines clanked in; they clawed and snarled, bucked and crawled, grunted and shunted, day and night, night and day. The hole deepened. In no time at all, workmen were going up and down on cable elevators.

Deep, deeper the Number One Dig went. The project had sound, top-secret backing. Huge amounts of money were shoveled in. The money came from somewhere, who cared where?

If here and there a media snoop stuck his nose in the wrong tent, he got clipped, but fast.

Now and then, a question surfaced from some weirdo muckraker. He was dealt with imperially, indignantly. "Question our president? Like asking God to turn out his pockets!"

Soundly, and as secret as God's pocket, the hole deepened. Under cover of night, families and all, more and more workmen were transported to the site. More and more scientists, sworn to secrecy and conformity, dealt with the complex questions which the hole, so to speak, raised; gravity, density, air, weather, and so on.

It was strange when you thought about it. (Very few thought about it.) The hole was top secret, yet everyone in the country, in one way or another, was in on the secret. A vast continental hole network spread. Few knew what they were researching, computing, deploying. Yet millions of people were being mobilized, taking their livelihood from a vast hole in the ground.

It was like a cornucopia in reverse. Out of the void came seemingly everything: RVs and cell phones and computers, and college for the kids, and designer clothes, and second homes.

And this being a religious people, it seemed only fitting that God be rendered thanks. So, one day a noted TV preacher was let in on the secret. Arriving at the site, the president himself welcomed him. The two shook hands fervently and were ushered onto the helicopter, Air Force One.

It buzzed mightily and rose straight up, steady as God's right hand. Then in mid air it veered and wheeled north and south, east and west; like a smart Christian insect, it traced a vast cross over the hole.

The preacher, a longstanding White House crony, was entrusted with the secret acronym of the hole: VOID, Veritably Our Identity Declared. "O, VOID," he intoned into the winds, a voice of silk and syrup, "O, VOID, bless us even as we bless Thee!"

Just like God, the Hole was thenceforth thought and spoken of with a capital letter.

Still and yet, blessing or no, it couldn't be said things were going well for the citizenry. A vague discontent roiled up in the land. It came from nowhere, it was everywhere. In point of fact, things seemed to get worse in proportion as the Hole galloped toward a world record and the economy quaked, the deficit soared, and the dollar sank out of sight.

Discontent and fretting gnawed away. "Why is gas so expensive? Why are trains always breaking down? Why does it cost so much to see a doctor, to die, or be born?"

Then, one day, terror struck. The Hole started to take charge. What had been a small mouth on the earth's vast face, a wrinkle, one declivity among many, suddenly seemed, overnight, a kind of stalking Grand Canyon. More and more earth caved in. Huge workers' camps collapsed and slid gently into the maw. Cars slid in, streets fell under, and hills folded up and fell like tarpaulins.

And yet, irony of ironies, the achievement was within our grasp. One more scoop, largely ceremonial! A hand was ready at the phone, the code phrase VOID IS US would flash over the hotline to the White House.

That Hole! It surpassed the Great Siberian Open Pit, the Mesabi Iron Range. It was deeper than the central valley of Switzerland measured from atop the Matterhorn, wider than the African plains from Nairobi to the sea.

The message flashed. The White House knew; the people did not.

But, but, the White House was locked down tighter than a maximum security prison.

Orders came down: no flags, no headlines, no TV specials, and no ticker tape parades. The president was unavailable. He was on his way somewhere else: he was in a meeting, any way you cut it. He would issue a statement tomorrow or the next day.

We had our world record. And everything was unraveling. The Hole was no longer a simple gap in solid earth. The rumor went around like thunder, like Armageddon. Planet earth was in danger of turning inside out!

Finally the President resurfaced. Haggard and sleepless, the famous artless smirk was wiped from his phiz. He called a midnight security meeting. The news he clutched in his hand was terrifying, his voice broke and shrilled in the telling. The Hole was becoming bigger than anything, bigger than the world. The USA would shortly be swallowed whole.

It was no time for buckling under. It was a time for bucking up, Founding Fathers, Higher Fathers, Emergency Management. The generals and PR types and handlers around the table stiffened their spines. All spit and polish, gruff, sleepless, humming with the power of positive thinking.

They took him on, head on. "No sir, beg to differ sir. Why, everything's under control. Granted, we've had a few flubs here and there, cost overruns, so on, granted . . . But who ever heard of the biggest job since creation not having its little ups and downs? Why we're flying a whole clutch of engineers down there, on twenty four-hour shifts, pouring concrete like crazy. . . . You'll see, we'll be hearing any minute now how the thing's stabilizing. . . ."

And the generals and PR types and handlers, statesmanlike and steady, peered into the middle distance.

The hot line rang.

The Vice-President leaned over to grab it. His face was unlike a Founding Father's, chiseled into the side of a mountain. But he was a seasoned pro, number one in charge of number one.

He listened. His eyes went blank. His face fell in like bread dough in a cold draft. The phone dropped and spun there on its cord. From the receiver they could hear a semi-articulate scream, as though a doll were being throttled.

Chicago was sliding into the Hole. Omaha was gone. So were the operators of one hundred thousand cement pourers, so were all the dozers, mixers, trucks, Caterpillars, and back-up crews. So was Salt Lake City. And just as the phone went dead, so went Minneapolis–St. Paul.

That was how it went.

The rest you know.

The day we won, we lost.

America Is Hard to Find

Hard to find;
    wild strawberries swans herons deer
      those things we long to be
    metamorphosed in and out of our sweet sour skins—
      good news housing Herefords holiness
      wholeness
    Hard to find; free form men and women
        harps hope food mandalas meditation
  Hard to find; lost not found rare as radium rent free
  uncontrollable uncanny a chorus
  Jesus Buddha Moses founding fathers horizons
  hope (in hiding)
Hard to find; America
    now if America is doing well you may expect Vietnamese to
    do well if power is virtuous the powerless will not be marked
    for death if the heart of man is flourishing so will plants and
    wild animals (But alas alas so also vice versa)
Hard to find. Good bread is hard to find. Of course. The hands
are wielding swords The wild animals fade out like Alice's cat's
smile Americans are hard to find The defenseless fade away like
hundred year pensioners The sour faced gorgons remain. . . .
But listen brothers and sisters this disk floats downward a flying saucer
in the macadam back yard where one paradise tree a hardy weed sends
up its signal flare (spring!)
    fly it! turn it on! become
  hard to find become be born
  out of the sea Atlantis out in the wilds America
    This disk like manna miraculous loaves and fishes
      exists to be multiplied savored shared
    play it! learn it! have it by heart!

Hard to find! where the frogs boom boom in the spring twilight
 search for the odor of good bread follow it
    man man is near (though hard to find)
       a rib cage growing red wild as strawberries a heart!
imagine intelligence imagine peaceable caressing food planting music
making
       hands   Imagine   Come in!
          P.S.   Dear friends   I choose to be a jail bird (one species is
             flourishing) in a kingdom of fowlers
                                          Like strawberries   good
                                                    bread

       swans herons Great Lakes I shall shortly be
          hard to find
an exotic uneasy inmate of the NATIONALLY ENDOWED
ELECTRONICALLY
                                    INESCAPABLE ZOO

          remember me I am
             free at large untamable not nearly
          as hard to find as America

                          —from *America Is Hard to Find*

A Dialogue:
The Good Samaritan

"That story, that summons
from thin air drawn, left hanging there—
summed up; the best and worst of us."

"Like the three sided character
stepping smartly toward Jerusalem—
of three irresolute minds—
would flee, would pause, would stop."

"I picture him, three or one,
jolting along time's track.
A clock strikes, ear cocks;
dingdongbell, one, two, three.
Priest, levite, outsider.
            Time's flummery,
ordeal dance; then
another bell, death knell—
near death in mid journey."

"Mere mockup humans, painted iron
tolling, telling, and all awry—
'All's well, God's world.'"

"We know it isn't—God's or well.
And what of the poor
wretch laid flat in the ditch?
Who's he? You, me?"

"Take it one further.
Those bandits
stripping the gospeler to his pelt
scuttling faceless off the page.
You, me?"

"Tell the time right!
It's not three of the clock
the somnolent hour, post prandial
post everything."

"Count the actors, a clue;
one traveler stripped bare, two
buzzing along, self important.
One pauses; importunate asks
What's going on here?
I count six hours, matin or compline hour.
Something ending or begun. But something."

"What make of one who makes
stories like that?"

"He's like a master clocksman, testing.
He's made time's figures—made time
Too—near nothing, mere something
the tracks, balances, wheels, bells had best
be obedient to."

"And we? Obedient or no?"

"Choice or mischance. He stands there
spinning the story; time's midtime,
time's end, no matter. Nothing's ended.
Those clock figures, trapped in time, let out
for merest show—"

"Christ plays in ten thousand places—
present tense, the big round number
laved in poetry; 'lovely in eyes
lovely in limbs not his.'"

"I dream sometimes, a sweet
revision and revenge
the robbers creeping back
shamefaced, giving over
rueful, their larceny."

"Mine is near nightmare, nightlong.
The scene; flat, edgy
a road named Chagrin. No terminus,
no origin. A smear of dust
dead as a snake's shed shin.
I muse on waking—the dream's about
trumpery eternity.
As though a snake of dust, its track
were all creation's story.
The snake vanishes, the road's a mere
base revision of our seven days.

Two walk that road, dazzled
with lofty pelagian fictions;
then, a slight discommoding.
As though the snake, trodden on, shuddered alive
throwing nice balance.
            Someone lies there
hapless, human. Trouble.
            A moment like a snake
invading, insulting the brain.
They pass by, hooded."

"You've not seen their faces?"

"I want to, I fear to.
            Is it want or fear
mounts that anonymous quick evasion?"

            —from *Jubilee!*

Blind

Scene: outdoor café, Athens. I: half in a trance under the merciless sunlight of noon. Good bread crunches between my hands, and a carafe of the tar-scented wine that keeps the gods bouncing back from Christian banishment.

Then this peddler of peanuts and chestnuts came in, blind as his wares.

He shuffled here and there among the tables, here and there, help of a sixth sense that more or less recouped the one he'd lost.

A strap around his neck supported a tray of his wares. And no one bought—no one—not a peanut. There was nothing here of sweet coaxing pressure, a prosperity that sends hands to pockets—something extra, a treat for the kids, why not, why not, he's blind isn't he.

There was little prosperity to speak of. The diners, the loiterers over cups of coffee, wine and bread, rarely a solid meal, it was here today maybe and gone tomorrow for sure. You saw it in the Sunday-best clothes, the best that is none too good, nothing shining new—and any article faintly summoning a Parisian panache long gone.

You saw it too in the eyes scanning menus, calculating, adding prices up, and taking their time. Just a hint of unsettlement behind the eyes and in the air. Tough times, bitter memories, the colonels only recently overthrown, post-tyranny, pre prosperity . . .

All sorts of weathervanes were turning in the wind, so to speak;

winds, rumors blowing this way and that, wayward. The weather was sunny and the air bright—but would it last? The cafés were open, a sign of confidence, nascent, vulnerable. It was like the first time a newborn child is carried out of doors for a viewing by friends down the block. You keep a weather eye out and oh, you carry the precious burden gently, the treasure it is.

"The way things are." It came together in a shabby street café. An observant eye in your head, the vendors spoke volumes—and the diners. You saw between the tables floating in mid air, mocking the good times gone, ghosts of big noisy five-tiered Greek dinners that were never ordered, never cooked.

Now and again the wind changed, it stilled on one side of your face and crossed the other, soothing, vagrant, a wind like a voice, a word soft as a wind. Touch of the good times! Thank you sir, thank you madame, here's your change, good day to you. The tail of the body economic wagging and wagging, the grin that seals the service, change jingling in an obsequious hand.

Nothing of this post-prandial satisfaction touched the blind vendor. He bumped his way, his stick tapping ahead, right, left, disconsolate among the tables. He sold nothing. It wasn't meanness; people simply had their own troubles to cope with.

In less cruel times—scarified as they are now by the lacerations of memory—the vendor would have been included in a large pervasive noisy familial aura of wellbeing, the Greek mode. Coins would have rattled in his tray of offerings. Here and there a chair would have been dragged to a table, the circle enlarged, him invited in. Waiter, a glass here, and a menu!

Memory is a cruel master; it wields a lash and the circle closes like a fist. So the blind man was dismissed, by common consent of the penurious. Eyes bored into the menus, hands pushed a knife here, a spoon there; attention went furtively elsewhere. He shuffled about, he was already elsewhere.

He sold nothing, or next to nothing.

Yet no denying it, he was a presence. He could (and did) lay a finger on an arm where you sat, like the flat thumbnail of death itself.

A summons hardly neither blind nor bereft of a sixth sense, a peculiar, piercing clutch of the hands of the blind.

He put a cold finger to you, without a word. His speechlessness was remarkable, it opened a void underfoot. You expected he would make up for his dead eyes with a lively tongue. Didn't those who plied the cafés owe something to the patrons, a minor cabaret turn, a witticism tossed over shoulder, harmlessly wicked?

Not this one. He stood there, a dumb stump of a man, wintry, a finger that turned you to ice. Nondescript in every respect, he could have been tossed together, a model and pattern set afoot in the world of a second-hand human, decked out in second-hand. A ho hum human—except for those eyes staring beyond and through, as though disdaining or dismissing you, or himself, or the world at large.

You imagined him biting the edge of a coin, or even the hand that tendered it; too little, too late, who needs you?

And he did—need us. The iceman cameth. His wares seemed turned to ice: to nails, hammer heads, buckles, cuffs, bars, metal teeth, fake icy chunks of jewelry, postcard views of Alaska. Death, he was death on the hoof.

Meantime, how were we faring under his stare, ranging widely, taking us in, in ways we had no way of countering? What was he making of this sunny, intermittently lively scene? A last meal on earth?

That blind desolating look of his, seeing everything or nothing—it was like the high piercing note of the end of things, it could strike and break the wine glasses to shards. The day was suddenly like a leaking carafe, the wine was spilling from full noon.

His circuit ended, he stood in the doorway for a moment, hovering over, registering, taking you in through his pores, through those interior eyes—eyes few ever open, short of the hour of death and amen. Short of that moment when the universe opens like an eye, seeing and seen, summoning and dismissing, and a coin is lowered on the sockets of the lucky blind and the sighted, alike at last.

The vendor stood there, his head turned about and about. He

said not a word. But he marked you. An X, like a tree for the ax.

Then he shuffled to the next table. A coven of young tourists, tired, vinous, bored stiff. A sharp word, they waved him off.

It was a last try. He turned full circle, found his direction. But in the clumsy sweep, toward and away, I swear he took a long blind look at me, my shirt and cheap pants, took me in, a god's owning eye. As though he saw what he didn't see? Then he was off.

I lost him among the strollers, the buyers and sellers, the hookers, the discontented, the enchanted, the locals and exotics, the big and little appetites, the little stores and their wares; ketchup, olives, fruits, cheeses, beer.

I lost him; he was cast like a blind cork into the turbulent flow of the street, corrosive and unremitting.

Maybe, I thought, his luck turned around, maybe somewhere down and away someone bought something.

Maybe, I don't know, he walked out of the world, having left his mark.

On me. See?

A Pittsburgh Beggar Reminds Me of the Dead of Hiroshima

Seeing the beggar's sign
lettered and hung like a sandwich board—
"I am blind, suffer from angina
and claim no pension or support of any kind."
the crowd dug deep, the tin can
sang like a wishing well.

These days, everyone being at war,
not to pay dear is to prod the inner horror
awake; speech starting up by heart,
lights going on and off, a Greek sky
where five stars make a god; a voice
we got them there; or he stood like a bastard here, but
we took him piece by piece;
shipped his skull home, polished like a gouty
whole head—

Perhaps the poem is odd man out
wherein my foulness
drags forward, touches His flesh
an emperor's birthmark
under beggardry, leprosy.
I am too unschooled to know,
befouled and blinded by the hot droppings
that struck my eyes in sleep, from the great bird
the descending fecal horror.
I stood and shook like ague
—Hiroshima, Nagasaki—

the ungentle names of my memory's youth,
the blue remembered hills
tipping like hell's buckets all their
hot afterbirth on me.

Healer, you would need
stout heart where I must stand;
no bones, nothing to start with
for repair and solace
of the vast meridian horror.
You would peer and poke
a blind man on a dump
tracing—another stone in a
dismembered wall—the Neanderthal
boy's bones, half discernible
in turned-up garden litter,
the obliterated dead, the slight
rhythms of marble tracery or flesh—which?

I believe in the Father almighty
and in Jesus Christ
his risen flesh, indistinguishable
from the permeating stench
that rises, spreads, drifts
on prevailing island winds
when a people goes up, a
mockup of city
slapped together for a brief
sequence—*lights, drone, target*—

Flesh of Christ—
indistinguishable, compounded
yeast, seed, flowering
of human flesh
your healing starts here
with the tears the dead
were given no time for, the living
numbed, no heart for.

You, Lazarus, who died and stank—
stagger like a zombie
out of the rubble, jaws
like a burnt carp, unfit for
speech or kiss, that fed
three days down, on carrion death.

Be first. Arise.
Teach the dead their discipline
—shank, hair, ear, articulation—
that rode like furies the inner seas
or fell
a dew on fleece, or settled
like sandman's gifts
on the eyes of sleeping children.

I toss a coin in the wishing
flesh of beggars; coins in the eyes
of murdered children, for buying of
no tears; a coin
in the carp's mouth for Peter's cast.

The dead too; my coin stand you in stead
who went improvident,
no staff or shift, into time's mountain
as though all
were wide door; this momentary hell
a heaven, and passing fair.

　　　　　—from *No One Walks Waters*

His Cleric's Eye
(G. M.)

A young priest, dead suddenly
at forty years
taught a metaphysic of the world.
His mind was lucid, ingrained. He would say,
it is deductibly verified
that God is immutable; and,
universal order converges on one being.

So be it. This priest, alas for poetry, love and priests
was neither great nor evil.
The truths he spoke
being inert, fired no mind to a flare;
a remote world order
of essence, cause, finality,
invited submission to his God.

He never conveyed a man, Christ, or himself—
His cleric's eye
forbade singulars, oddments, smells,
sickness, puchcarts, the poor.
He dwelt in the fierce Bronx, among a university's
stone faced acres
hemmed in by trucks and tumbrels. No avail.

Yet it could not be borne
by those who love him, that having passed
from unawareness to light
he should be denied
the suffering that marks man
like a circumcision, like unstarched tears; *saved.*
Heaven is everything earth has withheld.

I wish you, priest, for herald angel,
a phthisic old man
beating a tin can with a mutton bone—
behold he comes!

For savior,
a Coxey's army, a Bowery 2 A.M.
For beatific vision
an end to books, book ends, unbending minds,
tasteless fodder, restrictive order.

For eternal joy
veins casting off, in a moment's
burning transfiguration
the waste and sludge of unrealized time.

Christ make most of you!
stitch you through
the needle's eye, the grudging gate.
Crawl through
that crotch of being;
new eyes, new heart, the runner's burning start.

—from *No One Walks Waters*

Yes Is Yes and No Is No

Once there was a wise man whose tongue was stuck. When he wanted to say "yes," he said "no;" when he wanted to say "no," he said "yes."

Now all this hadn't happened overnight. When he was younger, he could deliver the truth like a straight arrow to a bull's-eye. It was "yes!" all the way; "yes" to truth and "yes!" to joy and "yes!" to love. And it was "no!" to hatred and "no!" to lust and "no!" to falsehood and "no!" to—but you have it, the resounding "no" to a black litany of our undoing.

Time went by, things changed. "Well things change, don't they?" he asked himself with a sigh.

Those who whizzed by in the fast lane, who traded and traded off, packaged and puffed—they thought of our man, some with envy, some with stark emulation. He was nothing short of Brightest and Best.

And yet, and once more—yet. He was too good, too near best, not to realize, when he stole a look into his soul, that he was nursing a catastrophe.

Years earlier, if provoked or aroused, he would have blasted out his "yes!" or "no!" like a very trump of dawn. Now it was a shrug, a "maybe," charming and empty.

His soul no longer struck a clear note, it was cracked metal.

Then quite suddenly one day, disaster struck. His tongue was locked in his head, his head locked out of his heart. He no longer knew "yes" from "no" or "no" from "yes."

Now what followed, may have happened—or may not. I can only report he said it happened. And since *something* happened—and since whatever happened changed his life utterly—but you be the judge.

One night, while he slept, a bird whispered in his ear, "Poor man, do you wish to untangle your tongue? To do so, you must travel over the southern mountains, must journey until you come to a wiser one than you. He will help; you will again come to know "yes" from "no.""

Now our friend may not have known a nod from a head shake, but he knew beyond doubt when a dream was real. He stretched out his hand in gratitude to touch the bird, which like any real bird, was no longer there.

He arose and voyaged over the southern mountains, first by moonlight, then by sunlight. Then there was no light at all. He lay down, weary beyond bearing, and slept. And behold, the same bird flew to his side, and spoke. "Your search is ended, and happily. You have come to the land of someone wiser than yourself."

The bird flew ahead; the man arose, walked and walked on. Presently he stood before a cave. In its shadow sat an old man, an ancient of days. He was planted in that spot from his youth. Indeed "planted" says it all; he had put down roots, sitting, sitting, sitting all his life. In that stony place, in all weathers, in all seasons, the days passed into nights, months into years.

At the start of his exile, thoughts of the past and uncertainties of the future fluttered nosily about his mind, chattering and bickering: "do this," "don't do that." In time, burdens, memories, prospects, all vanished. In a winged cloud, his former life swept past him, out to sea.

Thoughtful or thoughtless, he sat and sat, in the cave and before the cave. His face thinned to the bone, his beard grew, and it crept like a searching root into the crevices of rock. His eyes gradually closed, he hearkened no more to the sounds of this world.

Why he came there, whether he would ever depart from there, and whence—these were known, if at all, to God and himself.

Came our voyager. He sat down before the hermit; the silence enveloped him like a tide. It was as though the cloak of the solitary were stretched over him too, cherishing, welcoming the darkness.

Finally the voyager took courage, and spoke. "Help me, please help. I do not know "yes" from "no," or "no" from "yes." Out of the boundless world I have come to you, that my tongue might be loosened."

Nothing. Not a rustle of the cloak. Silence upon silence.

It was as though the voyager and his words were no more than a passing thought that, like a bird on the wing, sought entrance to the cave of the hermit's mind, or fled past, borne on a great wind.

Finally the hermit stirred where he sat. It was as though dark branches were shaken at midnight; and birds, snatched from somber dreams, fluttered about bewildered. The tone of the hermit was mournful beyond telling. "Maybe, maybe, maybe," he said. It was all he said: "Maybe, maybe, maybe."

Imagine if you will, the dire effect this had on our traveler, this "maybe" thrice repeated. To voyage so far, to leave all behind in search of a simple, direct "yes" and "no!" To be told by the voice of his dreams that a lost wisdom awaited him at the end of the journey!

Must he return empty of hand and mute of tongue, to his old life, to that land of duplicity and defeat, where "yes" was "no" and "no" was "yes?"

Had clarity fled the world?

He stood up. In his eyes dwelt the grief of mortals who wander and hope and knock; who are told: go there, come here, who see a door open, only to close again.

He rose and turned away, and went on, into the unknown. What else was he to do?

This time he walked into the northern mountains, first by sunlight, then by moonlight, then by no light at all. And he slept again, weary beyond recourse, and disheartened as well.

And behold in a dream, at his ear the same bird alighted—or one so very like as to make no difference. "Traveler" whispered the bird. "Listen. Know it or not, you have come on a bitter wisdom. You have learned that a wrong "yes" and "no" are not healed by a wrong "maybe." You have learned also that a wise man in trouble is not helped by a wiser one in trouble.

"Your journey is far from over. Beyond you must voyage, and beyond. You must cross a river that flows backward, a mountain that grows downward, and a chasm that looms upward. And at all times, you must keep your eyes fixed on the mirror I shall give you. Only through this eye, which sees all and is not seen, will you overcome perils and reach your goal.

"If you obey me, I promise: at the end of your journey you will meet the wisest man of all. He will at last unlock your mind and unstop your tongue."

Then the bird leaned close and drank the tear that stood in the eye of the wise one whose wisdom had failed.

The traveler awoke. The mirror, like any real mirror, lay at his side. And the bird, like any real bird, was gone.

He arose, and walked, looking steadfastly into the mirror. Many days and nights passed, much sorrow and weariness endured. He crossed the river that flowed backward, and lo, it flowed forward. He descended the mountain that fell downward, and lo, it grew upward. He climbed the chasm that towered above, and lo, it loomed downward.

Once more it was night, the moon rode high. For hours, footsore and near exhaustion, he climbed the mountain the mirror made. Up and up he followed the tortuous path.

Near the top of a saw-tooth ridge, he parted the brush, and found himself once more at the mouth of a cave. His heart sank, for the place was very like the one he had seen before.

So, too, the one who dwelt there. He seemed very like the maybe sayer; an old man seated on a mat at the cave's mouth. As the traveler drew near, however, he saw that this solitary was very unlike. He was as fat as the other was skinny, ample as the moon that shone above. In expression serene and inward, he sat there, face raised to the orb, as though he drank from its moony waters.

The solitary uttered not a word, whether of welcome or reproof. And all the while, as though his hands knew their task by heart, he busily wove rushes into a mat, taking form under his fingers.

Unwavering, his gaze was fixed on high, as though he were drinking from that old commanding orb, whatever waters or words, whatever silence, whatever phase.

What did he learn there, what did he know? The wanderer sat. For all the attention paid him, he might have been a night shadow among the shadows of rocks and trees haphazard lying or moving moonlit about.

Or perhaps in the mind of the hermit, our traveler existed somewhat as the moon itself, leaning and lurking, this way and that, and the shadows creeping after, that way and this.

❋

Hours passed. Thus the two lingered there, the old and the young. The moon waned, and then failed altogether. It was near dawn. The busy fingers of the hermit wove and wove his mat, turning it about as though he were shaking out its sheltering birds and flowers. The rushes whispered, parched, coaxed, and knotted in the old hands. It was a sound very like the rustling of birds in the wakening trees.

Morning came, bright and new. And still not a word from the hermit. Does he care nothing for living men, thought the weary traveler? Nothing for the bitter errand that brought me to so wild a place? Does he know? Does he not know? Why does he not speak?

The sun rose and blessed the earth. But the heart of the traveler sank into twilight. He sat there and he wept. What recourse remained to him, what was he to do?

Finally the spell was broken. A young man strode out of the cave. He was tall and straight as an arrow of willow, his face resplendent as dawn. The traveler looked up in awe, uncertain if he dreamed the sight.

Who can this be? Here surely stands no servant, but a guardian spirit of this wild place.

But what servant ever bore such a cloak about his body? Head to heel, the youth was resplendent in a cascading fall of feathers. More: he was crowned with a magnificent bird helmet—feathers, golden beak, eyes blazing as if with immortal life.

He carried in his hands a tray of fruit. He stood there for a long time, towering above the traveler and the hermit, a prince in his eerie. Then his eyes, lit by a life more intense than the fire of dawn, came to rest on the traveler.

The youth spoke aloud, imperiously. "You there, you must go! Our cave is not an inn; nor do we exist to offer refuge to the bewildered of this world.

"Don't you see?" he went on, and for a moment his tone softened, "We have nothing to offer you, your trouble and travail have been for nothing."

"For nothing, for everything, for a yes, for a no!" cried the suppliant in despair. "Have I come so far, do I stand so near? Is your master the wisest of humans, or is he a fool among men? Who if not he, can unlock my understanding, and give sense to my tongue?"

But the majestic servant turned, bent down, and set the bowl of fruit before his master. His cloak caught the fire of dawn; the colors flared like incense thrown on embers.

The traveler blinked and shied, as though he had gazed foolishly upon the sun.

The servant muttered: "What your plight may be, perhaps the angels know, or the eagles. What I know is simply told. The old man before you has been blind and deaf from birth. For ninety years, he has been fed and clothed and bathed by my two hands. And in all that time, he has never uttered a word. Wise he may be, or foolish, or something of both, what mortal can tell?"

Ninety years? How come, then, the servant had the look of youth, a face untried by the world?

Nothing. The mysterious servant stooped and peeled and broke the fruit. Half contemptuous and half tender, he placed the morsels to his master's lips.

And at that moment, the tongue of the traveler was unlocked at last, and his brain flowed free. In an onset of ecstasy, sweet to his hungering mind, he stood erect.

Then, as though his heart were calling a tune, he began to dance like a dervish in that high place. Turning, turning, an ecstatic blur. Finally he broke into a run, down and down the mountain, all but flying, heedless of the stony precipitous path.

As he ran, he cried aloud to the winds. "Yes, there is one wisdom only, and no, I have not known it until this moment! It is the wisdom of the hands that serve, of the tongue that forgets speech, of the silence that endures."

He passed the northern mountains; he traversed the witless landscape, the up that was down, the backward that was forward. He held no mirror in hand; everything in nature had turned about and righted itself. And he saw that the former land existed only in his bewildered mind, where "no" had been "yes," and "yes" "no."

He came at length to the southern mountains. And on the road ahead of him walked the maybe-sayer, the dour hermit of the middle journey.

On the road they met and embraced—the young man and the old. The hermit knelt. He sought healing of the metronomic "maybe" that so afflicted him.

And the traveler, his own healing fresh upon him, his mind singing out loud and clear, yes and no, like a bell tolling the time of the world aright—he stretched out his hand; and with a touch, healed the other.

It was like the first note of a new creation. A bell long silent, unsure of its true note, hung there in the dark. And then, and then—

The two walked on together, hand in hand, the old man and the young. They spoke rarely, but their speech was like the beat of bells, now one, now the other, now in unison, telling the time of the world—to, fro, yes, no, aright, aright.

Fidelity

Coming up Broadway, a fruitless evening
reception at U.N., the 'revolutionary ambassador'
resounding like a stale ash tray or like
the secretary of any state you mention & reflecting

sadly, the old game starts again
before the bloody flag is hoisted dry.
Life's an Orson Welles turn out of Graham Greene;

> The train rushes on, our hero in fatigues
> saunters down the careening aisle
> of the third class carriage
> expansive, macho
> he disappears into mirrors

> Minutes later he stands there—
> diplomat's stripes, strictly first class
> still as a sword cane. He's hardened, molten to mirror.

Alas folks, freaks, minority spirits, we've lost again.
It rains on Broadway, tears of knowledge.
I look for a store to buy a pen to blacken and blear
a page, tears or rain. I'll walk to 104th Street

where my old friend the picture framer
propped a photo of his dead wife in the window.

> Rain worsens
> Knowledge goes under

He was inefficient and faithful
she, propped in a wheel chair like a cauliflower
in a stall, months and months. Every hour or so

      lit a cigarette
      put it to her lips;

      One day
      a crazy old black woman
      named by me, Crazy Horse
      came by
      leaned convivially over

the speechless mindless creature, yelled
'How are you dearie?' and kissed her like a luv.

I've long pondered fidelity. You can't know
even Gerald Ford that lethal dummy, might be snatched
from mad comics by his cancerous wife. When the old woman
grew hopelessly ill, he closed the cramped
musty curiosity shop at 2 PM each day, took a taxi

      to Misericordia Hospital
      sat there at bedside
      all evening. One day
      slight good news;
      'She ate something, they've

.

stopped the intravenous feeding.' A merciful interlude only;
she died that night in his arms. On this foul foot path
mule track, death mile, oblivion alley, bloody pass
Broadway, pith and paradigm of the world, cutting the
50 States of Amnesia like a poisoned pie; a swollen Styx
an Augean drain ditch

       a lotus blooms.

He looked up grey faced as I came in. 'She went peacefully
your green plant was a comfort.' Still, wishing I could

                              summon

for myself, for my friends, someday

       for the world at large—
       yes the self damned
       the hypocrites, the power brokers
       the 'revolutionary ambassadors'

       a bare whiff of that bloom

hand laid on hand signifying a sacrament.

       When I edged in sideways
       past the morose dying
       woman, her wheelchair
       lodged like an embolism
       in the body politic,
       her skin
       wrapped like a rodent's
       in a moth eaten muff

I came not off magical Broadway
into Ripoff Boutique—
but where
springs have source

stream meeting stream signifying a sacrament.

—from *May All Creatures Live*

Certain Occult Utterances from the Under Ground and It's Guardian Sphinx

If you seek pleasure in everything
you must seek pleasure in nothing

if you wish to possess everything
you must desire to possess nothing

if you wish to become all
you must desire to be nothing

if you wish to know all
you must desire to know nothing

if you wish to arrive where you know not
you must go by a way you know not

if you wish to possess what you do not
you must dispossess

if you wish to become new
you must become as dead

—from *The Dark Night of Resistance*

A Penny Primer in the Art of Forgetfulness

What is the price of the future?
Forgetting the future

What is the price of revolution?
Forgetting the revolution

What things are to be forgotten?
The good things

Only?
Also the evil things

All things?
All things

What good things for instance?
Father   mother   family   friends

also books   tastes   a settled abode
the view at the window
ecstasy   flowers
the turn and tide of season

What bad things?
Offenses   hurts   foolishness   also
instinctive lunges   settled enmities
termites   rank offenses   shark mouths
the stuttering etc of nightmare

What is the value of this?
Connection

Where will it lead?
Forget where it will lead

You ask me to become a boor
an aardvark an amputee?
No. A Human.

How a human?
A human is one enabled
to forget
both method and way
            consumed
in the act & grace of the human
the entire gift

What gift act grace?
We must borrow
one outlawed debased word—
love

And then?
Then then then

Run off   empty your mind
like a dawn slops
or I shall I swear
by the Zen fathers
thwack your dense shoulders
with this bamboo

—from *The Dark Night of Resistance*

Eight Days in Sweden
(1974; the tiger cages, Vietnam)

Imagine; I'm the prisoners' public voice, I crawl like a bug up
& down the world's blank phiz,

shouting in stone ears. Yesterday in the Swede boondocks
marxists chomped their potatoes, watching with boiled eyes

me, sweating my soul for the lost tribes, the bones rotting in
Saigon cages.

Absurd theatre my meat, a dash of cruelty. I tell my soul;
don't turn intellectual mugger,
don't sweat despairing bullets in hotel rooms.

Believe, believe.

Believe? You're a lifelong slave, a dwarf
shouldering the scenery of some dark demonic scene;
you're

a brush in a pot of pig's blood, scrawling the title of a one
night stand named
'Candle In The Cave'; Or, 'The Bats Revealed As Right After All
Though Blind As Humans And Upside Down.'

Sweet distant brothers, sisters, save my soul.

—from *Diary of Sorts*

The Diggers
(of graves on the White House lawn)

having no future
which is to say
renouncing
all hardsell
trumpery and tricks

we strike free
for the work ordained—
digging in, in, in,
uncovering the dead
present, buried alive.

—from *Diary of Sorts*

A Sunday in Hell

ABRACADABRA intoned the Sunday preacher.

The pulpit looming high as a captain's poop deck; and below, the intent upturned faces of his congregation: menboys, womengirls, childdears.

ABACADABRA HOCUSPOCUS, WEAVE A HALTER, DEVIL CHOKE US.

DEVIL CHOKE US the preacher repeated, very fervent and red about the face, MALUS LOCUS . . .

Neither logical nor in any discernable sense scriptural, the sermon veered along, uncontrollable as a nor'easter. In style it resembled a kind of latter-day puritan histrionics, brought to the boiling point, simmering there.

Finally it played itself out, a rustle of garments and shifting of buttocks.

For his auditors, meaning and logic were not at issue. Nor was scripture. This was the sacred hour of the week; a matter of atmospherics, thunderbolts, a momentary spasm of guilt, paying up deliciously for the week's furtive backsliding, the wheeling and dealing . . .

After the service, the preacher stood as usual at the church door, receiving and dispensing greetings.

SPLENDID SERMON the menboys bowed.

THANK YOU FOR YOUR MESSAGE the womengirls smiled.

JANE, SAY HELLO TO THE REVEREND. DICK, PAY YOUR RESPECTS. FATHER, MEET DICK AND JANE.

At length the crowd dispersed.

THAT LITTLE BASTARD murmured the priest to himself as he made his way, sweaty and open-collared, through the empty church. DICK, SAY HELLO TO THE PRIEST. I'LL PRIEST HIM. THE LITTLE FART GAVE ME THE FINGER, STEADY ON, ALL DURING THE SERMON. HOPING I'D FORGET MY LINES, THE TROLL . . .

He retired early that night, muzzy with Sunday overwork (the big day) and a sheet or two to the wind.

And was plummeted into hell.

He knew it, he knew it, damnation, a matter of hearing, *fides ex auditu*. Schizophrenic, super sane, seventeen voices in his throat aching for release.

He stood in a sacristy of sorts. He looked up; a nun took no notice of him, she laced the altar bread with saltpeter.

HELLO HELLO a stentorian voice from the stone eagle in the cathedral tympanum, IN THE BEGINNING WAS THE WORD.

Fire struck his ear, a coal fallen red from the brazier.

The word, the word he was preaching, another voice, his own. His own! He was twisted around, his useless blind face turned to the wall, his back to the congregation; a windy word issued like paste from a tube—

And from his arse in evangelical heat, the word of salvation brayed, stertorous, murky.

The worshipers? They were stalled there, planted in the pews; an ambuscade of mutes, a nursery of propped-up embryos.

In hell, on earth, it was Sunday as usual. Logic was not at issue; in your sight this day, is scripture being fulfilled. Hell. The word, the eagle on the tympanum, comes home to roost.

The service ended, he stood as usual at the church door. The worshipers filed out.

Familiar congregation, familiar faces. Mr. Grimm's head was lodged in his collar like the business end of a hand gun. In hell he retained his profession: international arms trader, an office in which, in a former life, his skills had been highly regarded.

EXCELLENT SERMON he barked like a graveside salvo.

Ms. Grimm was no less remarkably altered in appearance. Her head was now the stick end of a broom. Self-propelled and obsessive, daily she swept their dwelling clean of infesting demons. Nights, she rode over the chimney pots of hell, one with her vehicle, medium, and message.

She muttered woodenly through some invisible orifice THANK YOU FOR YOUR MESSAGE.

In a former life the family had prayed together, right and just and availing.

In hell they stayed together, paid together.

Jane and Dick were two marmosets, on twin leashes. They were yoked like twin cyclones, red eyed, furry, leaping and crouching and snarling. A smart blow from Mr. Brown, and Dick, teeth snapping, hissed a HELLO to the priest. Ms. Brown struck Jane across the snout with a slack of leather. Jane snarled HELLO.

Forever it was as it had been. Sunday, church, family, worship.

The priest's recent indiscretion in the pulpit was drowned in winks and smiles and bobbing of heads; such things happen, the gestures said. Arse and mouth had corrected their embarrassingly mixed offices.

Why was it then, as the preacher regarded with stolid equanimity the altered form of his parishioners—altered and the same—the stone eagle set in the tympanum above, centuries old screamed, screamed in fury, vented in an obscene spurt upon his face and shoulders and the wind rose and the priest smiled and the throngs of the damned, worshipful as ever passed by in greeting and everything was as usual.

Then the wind rose in fury and he was stricken bodily where he stood, fell backward to the stone steps. Flattened there, he was transformed.

He became on the instant a smoke-blackened indecipherable blind volume, a bible in hell simultaneously burned out and sodden, with fires that consume not, waters that could not save page after page blowing away, wasted and dumb, bad news for good on the rising wind.

False Gods, Real Men

1.

Our family moved in 25 years from Acceptable Ethnic
through Ideal American
     (4 sons at war   Africa Italy   the Bulge   Germany)
and Ideal Catholic
     (2 sons priests   uncle priest   aunt nun   cousins
                           great-uncle   etc.   etc.)
But now; 2 priests in and out of jail, spasms, evictions,
                                 confrontations

We haven't made a nickel on the newest war
probably never again
           will think, proper
with pride; a soldier! a priest! we've made it now!

What it all means is—what remains.
     My brother and I stand like the fences
       of abandoned farms, changed times
       too loosely webbed against
           deicide   homicide
A really powerful blow,
     would bring us down like scarecrows.
Nature, knowing this, finding us mildly useful
     indulging also
     her backhanded love of freakishness
        allows us to stand.

The implication
        both serious and comic;
                wit, courage
        a cry in the general loveless waste
        something
than miracle
        both more and less

                        ... did conspire to enter, disrupt, destroy
                        draft files of the American Government,
                        on the 17 day of May ...
                                        —Indictment

2.

Among the flag poles
wrapped like Jansenist
conventicles
with rags
at half mast
(alas for sexual
mortmain) the wooden poles
on high but
dry

3.

We did yes we did your Honor
impenitent—
while legitimate cits
newts   bats   foxes
made congress
in formerly
parks and green swards
rutting   earnestly drilling
tooth and claw
galling   inserting
industrious   inventive
nitroglycerin, nuclear
instrumentalities

4.

We fools and felons
went on a picnic
apples   quince   wines   hams   swimsuits
loaves   fishes noonday relics and traces
badminton   watery footsoles   infants all
thereafter impounded!

> An FBI agent estimates at least 600
> individual files were in the two huge wire
> baskets carried from Local Board No. 33
> and set fire in the parking lot.
> —AP dispatch

5.

Then foul macadam
blossomed like rosemary
in the old tapestry
where unicorns deigned
to weave a fantasy
truer I swear than

6.

Judge Mace his black
shroud   his skeletal
body & soul
whose veins decant
vapors to turn the
innocent eye
dry as the dead.

When a Unites States judge sentenced
two of the pacifists to six years in Federal
prison . . . he clearly ignored sound dis-
cretion. The powers of the bench include
the power to fix sentences on those found
guilty, but they do not include the right
to impose punishment out of all proportion to the crime.

—*The New York Times*

7.

Indicted
charged with creating
children   confusion
legerdemain   flowers
felonious picnics.
Jews in Babylon
we sit and mourn
somewhere in Mace's
mad eyes' space

"I have tried all the conventional and
legal forms of protest to little or no avail,"
says Philip, who argues that both Christ
and Paul allowed the possibility of civil
disobedience when man's law counters
God's.

—*Time*

8.

TO PHILIP

Compassionate, casual as a good face
(a good heart goes without saying)
someone seen in the street; or
infinitely rare, once, twice in a lifetime

that conjunction we call brother or friend.
Biology, mythology cast up clues.
We grew together, stars made men
by cold design; instructed

sternly (no variance, not by a hair's
breadth) in course and recourse. In the heavens
in our mother's body, by moon and month
were whole men made.
We obeyed then, and were born.

—from *False Gods, Real Men*

Somewhere the Equation Breaks Down

between the perfect

(invisible, Plato said)

and the imperfect

that comes at you on the street,

stench and cloth and fried eyes;

between the wired bones of the dead

stuttering, shamed

and the marvelous lucid spirit

that moves in the body's spaces

a rainbow fish behind glass—

decide. O coincide!

—from *False Gods, Real Men*

Seminar

One speaker
an impeccable
Californian
impelled to explain

The Chinese Belong In China
The Russians In Russia.
we however—
messiah oversoul
a pink   muscled   clear-eyed
Texan dream
fumigating
Hanoi privies
from above—
napalm   jigger bombs   gas
God's saniflush, in sum—

The gentleman was
four square as State
or the pentateuch;
sans beard, rope sandals, foul talk, pot—
a fire extinguisher
on Pentecost day;
exuding good will
like a mortician's convention
in a plague year.

Indeed yes.
There is nothing sick
(the corpse said)
about death
Come in.

—from *False Gods, Real Men*

Diary (Easter, 1966)

I hadn't walked the tow path in Central Park
for six months, having flapped southward
like a lame duck under circumstances
that yield here to self-censoring.

I left; the Park gave scarcely a shrug,
the big body
autumnal, luxuriant,
a vague disinterest in eye
a hung up blear of smog
a rare fitful candor, a dog's
intelligence, an old horse's look. O sun!

Absent, the Park was in my heart
not noble, remorseful, remembering;
a wink, a New York shrug.
Nevertheless, went with me
an animal shadow, all its animals—
seals, weeping
the absurdest tears of all creation—

I called good night
the last time, November 20. The sea lion
a shmoo's dream of beatitude, a feast afloat
turned on me
his rheumy uncle's eye;
time for all that   time
to envy eagles, clouds like slow birds,
gulls slow as paper from the huffing stacks
time for return. He'd see me.

Southward, I thought of paeons to the Park.
Rio children had a park in mind
mud pies, dust cake, the hominoids like children.
Alas, their bones scrawled in the dust
alas, and the winds took the word away, as years
our bones

Home again, I visit the seal;
his majesty, cold in his ingrown mask
tight in his poorhouse trousers,
promulgates
the good life, laissez-faire,
49 brands of fish.

Ponderous
half in, half out of the water
his leather flipper
tapping the sea wall like God the Father
or Teddy Roosevelt
WELCOMES ME, NAME OF ALL!

O the Park descends on the city
like a celestial napkin, as if heaven
were all of earth, the fusty smell
of animals in arks, of cornered lives and deaths.
What is our freedom, Peter?
Obedience.
You have answered well;

I give you—exodus.
Wandering Jew
you have a Jew for God.
The Park
unreal as real estate
under the flood
bears you away, ashore:
The city!

—from *False Gods, Real Men*

The Skinless Folk and the Elbows & Knives Folk

O nce there dwelt, far from the stress and fury of the world, a race apart, a people fortunate in augury and origin.

They were peculiar (or peculiarly favored), in one remarkable respect. They dwelt in a climate perpetually temperate, an Eden of renewal and abundance.

You might conclude, if you were religious, that divine ones had placed them under an immense bell jar, for purposes properly divine, veiled from human understanding.

You might add, if you tended toward the cynical, that this paradise was a bit much, a dull setting for dullards. In that remote land, springtime perpetually followed summer. Then came a slight flurry known as autumn, a mere gesture, a desultory stroke of a brush, a hint of mauve where green had been regnant. Then spring again. No bite, no sting; and no relief.

The Greek poet Pindar anciently described them to a T:

Never the Muse is absent
From their ways; lyres clash and the flutes cry
And everywhere maiden choruses whirling.

They bind their hair in golden laurel and take their holiday.

Neither disease nor bitter old age is mixed
In their sacred blood; far from labor and battle
They live. They escape Nemesis
The overjust.

We spoke of a peculiarity. The word of course, hints at a bias.

Nevertheless, we report. Every spring, which is to say, every third, faintly shifting season, this people shed their skin. A people—except for upright form and skeletal structure—very unlike ourselves. For all but the faintest, most delicate membrane, they were entirely at the mercy of the world; its climate, fauna, flora, the very stones of the road.

Thus if every autumn found them in possession of a "skin," the thing is relative only to the condition say, of a newly hatched bird, or a fully ripened grape or peach.

But of what use was such a skin? They never thought to ask, any more than they asked: why are we not gifted with toenails like a sloth's, or body hair like baboons, or bony skulls like rhinos?

Indeed our calling them "peculiar" invites comparisons not altogether complimentary to ourselves!

In any case, spring was the dangerous season. It was then they stepped out of their skin.

Have you seen an eye out of its socket, or studied the veins and flesh of a grape? Thus, they, in the mild weather, like miraculous jellies, many hued. You see the muscles beneath skin, and the bones beneath those. Even more, you see all this in the motion and pulse of evanescent life.

One despairs of apt comparison. One has seen images of angels in the old chronicles; all those gleams, hues, glancing varieties. This people, too, made an epiphany, and for that, were all the more sharply and colorfully human.

It was also in the spring that their literature was written.

Swinburne and Tennyson were of the race of skinless poets, and the madman Chatterly, the Jesuit Hopkins. And in certain phases and moods, Shakespeare.

These poets were bewildered and saddened by the common lot. They were possessed by spirits. They raised their faces to the moon; the moon told them its lunatic secrets of rhyme without reason.

In the spring, skins were shrugged off, like tatters of seaweed on a shore—only multicolored. The skins lay there for a few hours; gradually they shriveled like seaweed or fine chamois or the petals of flowers. Then the discarded tegument faded away, or dissolved, or blew out to sea.

Nature had decreed that this people of necessity be peaceable. Constantly they must exercise care with one another: not to wound, to obstruct, to strike, to violate the vital jelly. So each kept at distance one from the other; they were temperamentally fastidious, skeptical, ruminating. Nothing swift, sudden, obtrusive! Their games were stately dances, to measured music.

How indeed was a culture to flourish when the precious brain and eye and testicle had no more covering than the skin of an eye or a grape? How indeed flourish, if that immeasurably thin membrane, delicate as gold leaf, were scotched each spring, leaving a people shivering before the faintest breeze?

Of course they made light of it, the danger and discomfort.

Year after year, the great cosmic cluster of skinless humans grew, ripened, and renewed itself under a sun as merciful and wise as the moon of Tuscany or the Tuscan grape.

Was there a fox in the thicket, whose teeth ached for that cluster? Alas, we are children of the Fall, no strangers to the question, or the dolorous evidence that urges an answer. The answer is compounded with our bones; it is the mortise of our being.

The question might be put in another, secular way. What brought this people to ruin? What was that "fatal flaw" the Greeks spoke of? Was this race akin to others, long disappeared in history— promethean folk, overreaching, covetous, violent, lustful?

They were not. How, then, was the human arbor wrecked, the cluster scattered?

It started with a supposition, innocent enough on the face of it. The skinless people thought they were the only tribe dwelling on earth.

This might be considered a tolerable illusion, implying no dire consequence if only—if such a people dwelt apart, or were adequately armed against the onslaught of enemies, or were skilled in arts and ploys of diplomacy.

Sometimes a great wall will suffice for bulwark, sometimes a great sea. Sometimes, a Machiavelli appears, and his devious hand holds back the deluge. And then, for a shorter period, and with vastly more ambiguous effect, a neutron bomb works wonders. And sometimes of course, nothing avails.

Alas, our Skinless Folk had, to their natural or inventive credit, neither wall, ocean, silver tongue, or bomb.

They accounted themselves religious, perhaps to a fault. I mean to this fault—a deadly innocence. They had no suspicion that at their borders lurked a running pack of foxes, fueled by voracious hungers.

This people, innocents all, looked to the wide heavens and invoked the gods. Their worship was esthetically beyond praise; it was moreover, infused with the faith that is said to work wonders.

That it worked no wonders for them, but to the contrary, immured them behind a tottering wall—this is explainable by a fault in their cosmos; a fault at once genetic and beyond repair.

To be sure, they invoked their gods. But the supplications were uttered in a bell jar, a soundless aural vacuum. Their gods heard nothing of entreaty and praise. And which gods, even the most beneficent, trouble themselves to read the lips of mere creatures?

So the rituals took place from an untouchable distance of unalterable eons, a kind of remote charade, a festival, or diversion. The gods, wrapt in the mists of whatever Olympus, sighed and turned over in sleep.

Then one day, as is recounted by the elders, a divine child, wandering alone in the eternal fog of the heights, grew curious. Who indeed were these remote creatures under the bell jar? He reached out, hefted the great knob and lifted the lid.

And the world rushed in like a wall of water against Atlantis. And that was all. Or so goes the myth.

Still, beyond the symbolism, a secular question remains, tormenting a secular age and its curious adolescent divinities. How was it that an entire people fell from grace, from history, from a vast promise, when, according to computers and calipers, such a people were destined to survive, even to prosper?

Through such instruments a conclusion stands; in our world, most people, thick-skinned or skinless, bony or obese, wall-building, sea-roaming, bomb-wielding—such people survive biologically, socially. They enter into the charade of give and take, dicker with one another, share tools and trades, and sometimes even mend their warlike ways— for a while.

Beyond doubt, at some point they make war again. But even in the renewed welter and chaos, something is gained, to the benefit of each adversary. The thick-skinned thin down a bit, the skinless grow skins. Or so the theory goes.

Computers and calipers failed to uncover the truth.

This: the downfall of the Skinless Folk came about in a moment through a massive invasion of their fair arbors. The invaders were known as the tribe of Elbows & Knives.

Their ominous arrival, together with the ruin they worked, is the stark, literal translation of the myth, the lifting of the bell jar.

Let us describe the invaders. The Elbows & Knives Folk were aptly named. They were skinny as blades. Or they had the clean bony look of shells found on beaches.

With a difference: this tribe could not, in any discernable sense, be "found" anywhere. They were restless, adroit, and ambitious; they zigzagged here and there about their land, about the world. They were, each and all, born fuglemen; and they knew it. Their image was a kind of blur in time and place. Indeed an old philosopher once described them as "knife blades pressed against the future."

That was it; they had no present moment. The only present they knew could be described as a kind of lifting or descending arc; the lift of an elbow, the fall of a blade. They were thirsty for the next step, the next shore, a refinement of invention, especially if they bent their minds to an instrument of violence. They dreamed of a better and bigger bomb.

They were consumed by the future, even as they consumed it like a wind, the wind of the vortex they created and rode. From frontier to horizon, from sea to shore to ulterior sea, they were perpetually exhausting and altering their own maps.

Happy—were they happy? The question would leave them speechless. Happy? They were on the move that was all.

Take for an image the thunderous arc, the five-thousand-mile annual trek of the African wildebeest, south to north, the length of the continent; the aged dying on the way, the newborn landing on soft hooves instantly in motion.

These people were like the wildebeest. "Move it!" was the national motto; and for once the motto stood true to the fact.

The Skinless Folk recoiled in horror. Surrounding them was a frenzied species, governed by no discernable law, intent on the disposal of as many enemies as might be inconvenient alive or exemplary dead.

Render as many as possible exemplary, subjugate the survivors; and then pass on.

However it came about (and here the stories diverge wildly, depending on the bias of academic majesties)—however it transpired, the clash was brief; and after a measure of sound and fury, inconclusive.

Many of the Skinless Folk perished, as might be imagined. It was as though a sharp blade cut with one stroke, the stem of a cluster of grapes. The Skinless Folk faded away. Skin and all, they were blown hither and yon, dissolved, taken by the sea in a cleansing tide.

A question that might be thought inevitable, never in fact arose.

What was the impact of the brief encounter between two such varied cultures? How—gifted as were the Skinless Folk in ecological finesse and religious rite, in literature and self-understanding, their culture limned in song, dance, and forged metals—how could they fail to dull the Knives, soften the intemperate Elbows? Contempt on the one side, innate over-bred shrinking on the other?

Let us imagine for a moment, an Elbow questioning one of those proud, finely nurtured, highly attuned folk: Who are your gods? How do you resolve disputes? Describe your mode of governance. Why do you carry no weapons?

Silence. No response. A wall of possessiveness: hidden jealousies brooding over a diminishing patrimony?

The brood hen, short of temper. If someone approaches, her head lowers, feathers ruffle, she settles all the more firmly on her nest. (If she only knew it, her eggs are sterile.)

Under occupation, the Skinless nursed their bootless pride.

Granted, they had at their disposal mantras, poems, myths, grand music. Their sensibility was marked by rapture, compassion, magnanimity. They were fabulists, recondite and elegant.

They were also inbred and jealous.

If a questioner (in their eyes, a tormentor) approached, they withdrew into moody silence, without issue or logic.

The Elbows, be it understood, were not arbitrarily cruel. They were easily bored, that was all. After a while, being undeniably in command, they freed their impenetrable captives, and passed to other interests of the moment.

At the time they were preoccupied with preparations for a moon launch.

The myth put the outcome in another way, as we have seen. The gods grew weary of their pastime. In an idle hour, one of their kind raised the knob of the jar and thrust the sharp-faced fox into the grape harvest. The fox sniffed about, looked up longingly once or twice at the high and mighty prey, grew bored and loped off. No contest.

Once more a bell jar lowered on the tribe; a smaller one this time, in protection of diminished lives.

Thus the myth defined the fault, and the consequent fate, of our Skinless friends, who perhaps did not dwell very far from here.

They lost touch, it was said. They lost interest in the outside world; which in consequence, took its revenge, losing interest in them. An unspectacular outcome. It was rather like the rotting of grapes underfoot, a sharp momentary odor, pungent with memory, perhaps with regret; then nothing.

The myths, be it noted, dwell upon the downfall of one tribe. In so concentrating, they by no means advocate the methods or ethos of the Elbows & Knives Folk. To the contrary: a judgment is implied. They are accounted a repulsive fraternity, ruthless in their conduct of affairs in the world.

Not for nothing, their name.

Elbows are useful anatomical appendages surely, allowing for outreach and versatile gesture. Who would willingly be deprived of them?

But these people, as the tale indicates, transformed a tool of nature, a thing, into a very verb, a mode of action. Thus they spoke of "elbowing one's way," "elbowing ahead", "elbowing someone aside". Such phrases became an odious cover for a competitive existence. In it, the devil takes the hindmost.

Given time, the tribe became in a sense all elbows, every human trait subject to the spurt and spoils of ego, greed, ambition.

Let us also pay due praise. The Skinless Folk people found themselves elbowed aside by a slashing storm of goers and getters. And the victims seldom showed irritation or animosity.

For this, one is inclined to praise them—to a degree.

As to the question of Knives. Again, one could register no great objection to such tools, in their proper and modest place. Bread after all requires cutting, surgery is a useful skill, as is woodcarving.

But the Elbows & Knives Folk people are hardly content with such instrumental modesty. What, they asked, could be of greater usefulness, by way of warning or defense, than our knives? In such a world as we must inhabit, what people would deprive themselves, out of misbegotten idealism, of the simplest means of self defense?

Bigger and better knives, was the cry. Night and day, the forges burned and winked, the sparks flew from the wailing emery wheels.

Inevitably, in virtue of an edgy logic, the Elbows & Knives Folk came more and more to resemble their tools; which in time became something other than tools; more like weapons.

As weapons sharpened, it was remarkable how sensibilities dulled. The Elbows & Knives Folk no longer shuddered at their "necessary" bloody activity. Now it was a shrug of the shoulders, a roll of the eye, an equivalent "what's the problem?"

At that point, a Shakespearian futility: "What's done is done, and cannot be undone!"

One recalls the fault of the Skinless Folks—ennui, disinterest in the world, consequent loss of touch. Their thoughts were airy, and in time became airborne.

One is uncertain whether to name the fault moral or intellectual. Indeed the distinction may be without significance.

According to our story, the world is not long indifferent to those who scorn her joys and agonies. A mysterious court of accounting was convened. It was (and is) untouchable by rancor, ideology, or earthly appetite. From its deliberations flow whatever of justice remains in honor among humans.

From the court in due time, a summary verdict: the Skinless Folk were judged irrelevant to "the world, the way it goes."

The outcome was not so much a condemnation, as a simple announcement of fact. And this was the cruelest cut of all.

The tribes of earth, wherever dwelling, weave and ravel their own fate. But they weave blindly. They see only the immediate detail of pattern, nothing of the grand design of centuries, where wise or errant choices lead: choices that reach forward and back, like the hands of the unborn and the dead, in their turn also weaving and raveling, raveling, weaving.

Thus the judgment. It proceeded, as was insisted, from something known as the nature of things. It was like the precipitous descent of winter upon a Folk who could flourish only in the sunniest, most soothing clime.

A curious event and natural: night frost and morning snowfall. But it was brutally final. The Skinless Folk succumbed.

Thus the two tribes saw themselves and thus were seen, worlds apart in defining the same world: the Skinless, the Elbows.

And whence, from whom—storytellers, gods, stricken mortals, aggressors, survivors—from which of these might come the truth?

This is the function of the spinner of the tale. He need not elbow his way in, anywhere. He belongs to time and this world, is indigenous to every tribe. Nor is he to be cowed or put in "rightful place," not by a very regiment of Elbows, an assault so overpowering as to seem an image of an assaulting universe.

Nothing of that. The storyteller possesses three or four dull knives, laid away in a kitchen drawer. The tools stay put. They are never transported for any reason, including the universal folly and fiction known as "legitimate defense."

By way of objection it might be adduced by the unprotected Skinless, that the storyteller is a special case. That his skin is a resistant tegument, that it has survived the abrasive nicks and carvings of the Knives of church, state, prison, courts, universities, and other notable Defensores Legitimae.

Let the scrivener for a moment, become somewhat odious. Allow him to describe his unease with the theory of Middle Ground.

He thinks he is not required to choose between being Skinless, and being armed to the Elbows. There are, he believes other and better ways available to us humans.

Indeed, he hesitates to honor either of the tribes by regarding them as sane alternatives. He is convinced that the tribes are themselves aspects, even embodiments of the same culture. And to that degree, both tribes are fated one day to hear pronounced against them a like judgment.

The storyteller ponders the above, and is not happy with the timing, "one day." Grant him a second thought. He is convinced that the judgment is already promulgated. It works its relentless ways, like an immortal worm through a rotting fabric, ingesting all—even as it retains in itself whatever immortal residue and essence.

Elbows & Knives Folk, one notes, can hardly be accused of indifference to worldly matters. Indeed, the opposite is true. They are a people of voracious interest in the world and its goods, services, markets, incomes, investments, politics, potential. And all, alas, for no commendable reason: for possession and control, a condition diagnosed here and there as a disease, and rightly.

The Skinless Folk, as already indicated, express an attitude almost equally disastrous: indifference to the prospering or withering of the world Vine, or the people perilously and fruitfully appended.

Both tribes, insists our necromancer, embrace an ideology so strongly imbedded in the respective lines as to become biology; and to that degree, even a kind of destiny.

A confession is also due. The storyteller is not certain he can sustain the fiction undertaken here. His story, in fact, has nearly and awfully come true. He is afflicted daily with a sense that the fictions are bearing him away, afar. And worst of all, he has scant knowledge of the way of return. Does he walk in the daylight or does he live in a dream within a dream? He is not always certain.

Does there exist a third way? He longs to believe it is so.

More: he is certain that the so-called first and second ways are in fact, one and the same. Skinlessness is a kind of weapon; and Elbows and Knives are the armature of the ethically skinless. Can one simply say to some: drop your weapons? And to others: grow a skin? The first seems a command fairly simple to obey. But the author submits that it would be contra naturam for the Elbows to drop their Knives, to discard their bombs: Tridents, Peacekeepers, Warthogs, Cluster— as it would be for others to presto! create a skin, whole and entire, thence to walk in the frigid and torrid world.

To flourish there?

The storyteller is perhaps pointing, not to a failure of nerve, but to something deeper, more ruinous: a failure of moral imagination, a drought and dearth of alternatives, a well gone sour, or parched— but in any case empty of usefulness or delight.

His tale also mourns the forgotten skill of a tradition named community. The forgetting of which is, as far as he can understand, an aspect of death.

He is haunted by the blown skin, the hapless and naked, as by a knife lodged in a stopped heart.

My Father

1.

All bets were on; he was dying
back in '62; found by mother 2:00 a.m.
on the john floor, bleeding end to end mightily.
Toward dawn I was summoned;
A jungle of tubes and bowls; going out big,
the symbols of mortician culture
blooming around like fungi.
He lay there weak as childhood.
They were filling him, an old sack,
with new wine. He took it darkly.
"When the wheat's ready for harvest,
draw it in," all I remember.
Strong enough behind his milky cat's eyes
to spin trope about death, strong enough to live.
Foul January dawn
beetled down upon us, he lay there like a switchblade
awaiting the spring, awaiting death
like a palmed blade. No takers . . .

2.

Phil goes in chains to Harrisburg today
I sit here in the prison ward
nervously dickering with my ulcer
a half-tamed animal
raising hell in its living space.
Time to think once more of my father.
There were photos, brown, detailed
tintypes. You had only to look

(30, 40, years ago)
for the handsomest bucko present.
It was uncanny.
A head of burnished locks, a high brow
a cynic's sidelong look.
Boyo! You kept at center eye
the eye of storms.
In a mad Irish way "all there." Whole apple, one bite.
The mouth reminds me of a whip;
sensual and punishing.
Tasting the world, sexually alive,
calling the tune, paying the piper.
He was chaste as an Irish corpse,
Mother-maidensister-haunted.
We 6 were as much emblems of expiation
as of seasonal bedding
each of us sponsored by the church
like a first class relic or a nun's goody.

3.

I wonder tonight in Danbury Prison
in the damned off-season of human beings
an ulcer kicking at my groin
like the sour embryo of Nixon's next brainchild
I wonder—
the Jesuits staring 'round like frogs of the Nile
at baby Moses—
I wonder if I ever loved him
if he ever loved us

if he ever loved me;
an undersized myopic tacker
number 5 in pecking order
pious maybe, intelligent I guess
looking for corners where half in, half out
he could take soundings,
survive, emerge; protective coloration.
Not enamored of the facts of life
i.e., sledgehammers, chicken little,
the cracking muscles of the strong.
As a child you expect violence; the main issue
somehow to clear away
space and time
to survive in. Outside the circle, who cares?

He exacted performance, promptitude,
deference to his moods
the family escutcheon stained with no shit.
The game was skillful (we never saw it so well played
elsewhere), he was commonly considered
the epitome of a just man.
We sat on our perches blinking like six marmosets.
There were scenes worthy of Conrad,
the decks shuddering;
the world coming to end!

He is dead now.
The conduct of sons and priests
is not grist for news-hawks and kites.
When my mother (who surely
suffered most at his hands) read one account
served up by an esteemed scribe

she wept for shame and loss.
There is more honor, more
noblesse oblige, more
friendship with reality, more unconscious graceful wisdom
in the least gesture of her
little finger, than in
the droppings and screams of the whole preening profession
of whooping cranes.
The office of charity, of classic
Pietàs, fills the vacuum
around that absent figure
with the presence of compassion. My father—
when in '39 I braced and dug in
for the great leap, I was one
of 38 candidates for priesthood.
All excelled me
in arts, language, math,
self-assurance, the golden number of
the Jesuit dance. 32 years later
I sit in Danbury Prison for illegal
acts contrary to war.
Father
I close my eyes, conjure up
like a deaf-mute mimic
your ironic ghost. How convey
my gratitude, my sense
of the delicious rightness of things?
Whatever you denied us, you
gave us this, which enemies name
distemper, madness; our friends,
half in despair, arrogance.
Which I name, denying both—the best of

your juice and brawn, unified
tension to good purpose.
Prosit, requiescat.
The bad news drones on
plague after seventh plague
hypnotic, futile as an argument
for God's existence. . . .

5.

. . .
My father, asked what crop he grew
on the old farm outside Syracuse (depression
sour clay and drought); laconically:
boys! One year, an old mare dragging a harrow
through the sparse corn rows, with the perfect timing
of senescence
reached a drain ditch
near the roadside, stepped down daintily
as a duchess, lowered her backside,
lowered her long face to her knees (harness
jangling like rude jewelry) lay there
saying from her eyes; next move, yours.
Tonight under a paschal moon, I mimed
a Goya etching in the
prison yard
3 shadows coming, growing
came, grew, vanished like footpads—
Jesus, Satan, that interdicting
third, weaving, bargaining, up to his ears
in bloody Friday; Lord, is it I?

Under the shrewd exhalation of the moon,
I bundle up to throat; no
horse thieves, poachers,
informers in our blood! Nicked by his razor Dado
mutters in the mirror; *the blood of Irish kings*!
Mother at the stove, turns up her eyes to heaven . . .

7.

Dado's classical bent
left none unstigmatized. A white billy-goat
was marvelously misnamed, to fanfare
from the dog, faint horselaugh from the mare;
Ursus. He knocked the postman for a loop,
scattered mad Mamie Powell, chewed up,
in the side yard, until chased by sticks,
the shirt the '29 depression spared.
Crimes multiplying, stink
offending, he was sold off, reversing
the Judas trick, to metamorphose in paschal stew
in Little Italy, down country. We mourned him—
hooves, pride of blood, horns of
neighborhood dilemmas, nattering mouth, pirate's eye,
the uncouth unreconstructed thieving
alter ego of six boys.

1930; Dado decreed a mercy death.
A splay-legged spavined nag
bit the dust, under an orchard tree,
Tom firing point blank. Laziness
our virtue in common; we dug a shallow grave

heaped the cadaver over, like a
prairie cenotaph. One week later, mother,
stringing the laundry from tree to tree
was shaken to tears and flight. A colossal
long drawn fart issuing from the grave,
a strange unnatural
convulsion; earth heaved ground opened,
a great equine rear leg shot up skyward.
The resurrection of the dead?
Weeks passed, sweet seasonal process
grounded the upstart sign, grounded my father's
Jovian lightnings . . .

8.

     In the old fables
  jays   macaws   jackals
cowardly   inching forward   careening   hobbling   jeering
  surrounded the mysterious firebird
  The figure and form of the age.
Philip; the little blond boy with lowered eyes
    in a blue fluted sweater
       stands to the left of me in a faded Kodak film, 1927.
  You threw stones like a demon
   hid your windup locomotive in the old grey immigrant trunk.
  In one year your limbs telescoped out
    a poet's brow, those commanding utterly blue eyes
  a sapphire intensity, precision instruments taking
    the world's size.
   I do not know when the wager was first struck
  I see another photo, a windy June day

    outside Washington Shrine, the family smiling,
  a single-minded triumph; its ordained priest!
    war years, depression years   decently buried in albums
then that "stampede into religion"
        (John's sneering phrase)
    the church's chased cup
continuity, rounded latinate
        breaking up   breaking up

Dado,
your sons
close kept in Danbury Jail
keep Maundy Thursday.
You lie close too
after the 90 year uphill climb.
Pompey graveyard, a "sylvan close"
(your phrase) of trees and mounds
slopes westward, gentle, sunny.
Are you proud of your 2 priests
plucked by the sovereign state, for crimes
against war crimes? The children of My Lai
like Fra Angelico's angels, make sport of death;
with instruments of harmony
keep green, for us, your grave.
Children—those natural buds
those nodes of process, rose red, snow white
first fruits of blood and semen, fallen rosy and white
to the spread aprons of women, fruits
of energetic love. Who strikes them— . . .

10.

Winters we chugged two miles to Sunday Mass
in a model-T snowbucker, old the year
   it was born. Like a sailing fish it sported
flapping gills of isinglass and canvas.
   We bedded down like Peter Rabbit's litter, crowded
in the hold, eyes, cold noses, Dado
   pumping and worrying us along. Spread over all
6 boys, a 7 foot square Buffalo robe
   gamey, coarse as porcupine. Arrived, dismounted
at St. John Baptist
   we made an obedient huddle, awaiting
disposition of the steed. The robe, pulled from the rear seat,
   made a splendid radiator noseguard
against deep freeze.

   We sat at the children's Mass
singing from 5¢ notebooks the hymns
   we murdered all week to Sister's beating stick
Mother dearest Mother fairest; to Jesus' heart all burning.
   Monsignor McEvoy, our ample prophet, out of his
workday overalls (teacher, lawyer, builder)
   splendid as an iconostasis, humble as Nazareth
gave us a children's gospel. Not bad; religion
   stuck to our Sunday bones . . .
If we went mad, it was
for sweet reason's sake;
to wish all children well; to make of the world's breakup
cup, loaf, murder, horror, a first (or last) communion.
                              Once a year
   New Year's Day, Mom and "the gang"
(Maggie's put-down) were summoned
   to state dinner. I remember

straight chairs, straight talk, kids
    frozen to our seats by the old maids'
steely looks; indifferent food, Maggie
    dispensing into shirt pockets, on the hour
with a teaspoon, her stony pacifier, "Loft's Hard Candies."
    They were straight out of Port Royal, Maynooth,
Oneida, pure as angels, proud as devils.
    My father's marriage stuck in the throat of virtue.
Upchuck or swallow; the discreet dilemma
    was audible for years, burp, cover up.

Grandmother Berrigan's portrait
    looked down in mild wonderment,
a queen above a nest of bickering kites
    she, troubled, questioning
the trick and treat of time's outcome—11 children, a widow on
    Christmas day
        of '74. Grandfather, bleeding
from immigrant's lung,
    A daughter ran outside
to break the ice on the rain barrel, plunge a chunk
    into his mouth. His body hauled
up scoured December hills in a democrat wagon
    to lie where my father would lie.
Dado slept that day, a child
    in a farm woman neighbor's arms . . .
I set this down
    in Danbury Jail; Philip and I
priests, first (for all we know) to break
    trust of the clan, trust

again and again, like Jansenius'
    first rule of order; first pass-fail;
no one, not one of the
    family, ever in jail.

11.

In old Assumption church on Salina Street
a phony dungeon on the dark rear stair
kept con Jesus under lock.
We crept down
during the long noon hour,
Lucifugae, sprats, beguiled
by darkness and vigil lights, prayed there
some better outcome for the man, caught in the twin
pincers of church and state. Would Pilate
dash the bowl to the ground, would Caiaphas convert? . . .

Holy Saturday I set this down
by courtesy of the twin powers, doing time.
Jesus, lift head tonight from the foul grime
of churches. Thorns like bees
drone at the skull; does sacrifice bring in
straight on a beeline, honey, money, honor?
The dull eyes focus under a full moon
outside my window, resplendent
to frame a face in the informer's kiss. Who knows? Who knows?

a bargain struck
in silver, brings it down; rain, ruin
piece by piece, indictments on the 6
Harrisburg peacemakers, Berrigan et al
versus United States . . .
My grandmother's head
turns side to side, dubious as a ghost.
We teased mother.
Tom, Tom, the farmer's son,
why did you ever marry that one?—
(she blushed)
Indeed? He was considered quite a catch!

12.

November dawn, 1969, your jaw dropped, a semaphore
        the last train out of ghost town.
We gathered in 2 brown sacks
        everything you owned, an immigrant pauper's bundle

I leaned over the bed, breathing for you
        all that night long
        (somebody else was there)
        2 shadows over a fish tank
        helpless as men watching the death
        of the fish from whom
        all men, fathers and sons, ad infinitum, come
A fish metamorphosing
        into a father before our eyes—
        hands, feet, blue as a fish

I could not take you in my arms, give you back
    wits, volatile energy
    confounding moods, appetite
    the farm, drought, depression years
    the scythe that whistled
    like a wood plane across hard earth

Did you want it all back anyway?
    Think. 6 sons, 5, 4, 3, 2, 1,—
    then nothing, a wedding night, a bride
    life awaiting doing all again?

You hated like hell that necessity
    we lived by—your scant love
    the stigma
    it took years to heal; making do,
    fear, damnation, fury.

Well we made it; some deep root of sanity
    we sucked on. Above,
    the idiot thrashing storms you made

Maybe it was your face dropping its mask
    asleep over a book,
    Irish intelligence; now and again
    a piercing stab of virtue; a boy
    kneeling beside you at Mass; a 6 yr. old
    rocking-horse Catholic.

Thank you old bones, old pirate
    old mocker and weeper.
Could have lived to a hundred. But contrary passion
set in hard; falling downstairs
that last time, into your own
unconscious. To hell with it; bag it all.
a bloody act of the will, a fever nursed by rage. Sons
no longer mitigating presences, who
now and again had been;
    has been now. You turned to the wall.

And I have no recourse except
hatred and love, your hand
breaking through the earth
nightmare or miracle;
your face
muffled in its shroud
a falcon
disdaining
the dishonor nailing
us here like stinking fish
(ancestors, sons)
to the world's botched cross

Landed, boned, buried in Pompey yard . . .
To see the performance, was scarcely
to believe it. One summer night
he tipped
the kitchen table, set for supper, up on end
for some supposed infraction. He fought sons

to a sullen draw, told enchanting children's stories
of summer nights, wrote poetry
like a flaring Turk, absurd, byronic,
battled the land to a dust storm,
prayed, slept stertorously in the big
leather rocker, ate like a demon,
exacted instant "yes sir! no sir!"
died like a sword swallower choked on
his breath's long blade . . .

The old house breathed relief
in his absence. None of us could, those years,
were screws turned on our thumbs, confess
to love him.
Was it that dearth of love
turned us to the long tragic way
on and on? What measure
of that irascible spirit, lodged unappeased
in us, bears, endures, survives—even Danbury? One virtue awaits
the arresting fist of death.
Until: Walk on, Take breath, Make do.

In blinding Minnesota winter sun
one of the older brothers
would hoist a kid up, pick-a-back, and run.
I was 3 or 4; John trundled me round the yard
ducked suddenly into a dark wood shed
striking me blind. Against my face
some rough pelted thing swayed frozen.
Recovering sight

screamed, screamed like a banshee, a child
gone mad for terror;
a frozen timber wolf's death-head
hung by a thong from the rafters, eyes open
bloody mouth—

    The stuff of nightmares or of dental chairs.
  In Danbury Clinic
I urge the wary inmates; *open wide now*; a superannuated
  paraclete, all in white
for the liturgy; needles and drills
  needles and drills. Domestic policy, we juice
America's pain to sleep

In the wink of an eye, graves shall open
the dead arise. Easter morning
I write: dearest mother, many friends
bring flowers to your bedside, smiles
from Danbury. We are well, our thoughts
are thanks. Thanks to you, the instrument
of truth, who plucked us by the hair
harebrain and all, from false peace. Alleluia.

              —from *Prison Poems*

The Committee and the Camel
or *How a Famous Bishops' Letter on Nuclear Weapons Came to Be*

L et us imagine, for the moment, that the days of creation have gotten turned around—in this wise. Humans have been flourishing for some time, but many animals have not yet made an appearance. Nor has the sin called "original" been perpetrated. In fact, the world is considered by all concerned to be in reasonably good working order.

Still, something was missing—the animals.

A committee was therefore summoned with instructions from on high. They were to help the Creator resolve the animal question. The mandate was summary; the committee was ordered to put together something never before seen on land or sea. "Let's call it something like 'a camel,'" God said. "You bring me the working blueprint, I'll produce the beast."

The committee was nothing if not inclusive. Summoned were the honored and learned, the staid and venturesome, even a few demurrers and doubters. They came together; for weeks on end, sweating away, studying and stewing, discerning and argufying.

Hour after hour, day and night, they sought hints from the other fauna that might shed light on the elusive camel. From aardvark to zebra they paraded the beasts, visited zoos, embarked on distant safaris.

The task was daunting, frustrating. "What the hell does a camel look like?" one of them asked one day. "How are we going to produce one if we've never seen one?"

Their leader was irked. He looked up warily from the encyclopedia where he was researching his assignment for the day: armadillo. "It's not a ques tion of whether someone has seen a cam el or not," he said between set teeth. "Don't you know what faith is, the sub stance of things un seen?"

He was inclined to push orthodoxy. If the committee got out of hand, his status—interlocutor, ombudsman, whatever, someone who must take fools and saints in stride—these might get clouded.

"We don't want any muttering around here." He looked sharply around the table. "Just open the book of Exodus, you'll find out how far murmuring gets people."

They went on sweating and discerning; the camel slowly took a cloudy form. Someone came up with a hump, another with foot pads, another pushed for rubber lips and a disdainful eye. Then for a while there was smooth going, agreement on storage tanks, low literacy, and bad temper. After a particularly punishing day, with only an edge of ill feeling, they agreed that flatulence must be tolerated, a lesser evil.

They also began to see their own limits. "We've got to get some expert advice on this," one of them fumed one day. "We've got all the parts," he gestured wearily toward the Himalaya of papers in front of them. "But they just don't add up. What are we going to submit to Quality Control, a Disneyland mutt or something?"

The committee agreed, the experts were summoned. One after another they came, trailing their graphs and sketches and charts and slide projectors—oceanographers, cartographers, ozone sniffers, spelunkers, futurologists. There were Eskimo experts and Amazonian experts and Patagonian experts. There was a hirsute speechless type who had dug in for a lifetime in the upper reaches of the Orinoco. There was a mealymouthed hustler who sold used cars to Stone Age Indians. They came in with lean and hungry looks, each saw his chance to peddle his own camel.

The first to speak fixed an inflamed eye on the committee. He talked about flippers and flab, flab and flippers. The camel must, above everything else, be oceangoing, a cousin of the burly sea lion of the Bering Straits.

Another, an inflated ego fresh from a right-wing think tank, spoke through clenched jaws. There were, he declared, bigger and better camels already in possession of The Enemy. "This I'm qualified to say only in these four walls, strictly classified. Right now, while you true believers sit here splitting hairs, we have incontestable info—Bin Laden and his slimy crew have a long-haired long-horned herd of camels stashed away in Upper Mongolia just waiting to mount an attack on the One Indispensable Nation.

"An' you sit here. An' sit. I happen to know the timetable you were given; three months you've been at it, an' not so much as a reasonable facsimile."

A bad day. But there was worse to come.

A military type stalked in. He was promoting a kind of armadillo camel, a defensive offensive beast. Top-secret government priority.

The beast was adaptable, it was feasible, it had a rear end capacity to turn about and become its own front end, and vice versa. A surprise factor built in: "bewildering the enemy beyond recovery, and lending the beast an unheard of first strike capability."

The wonder camel was of course far ahead of anything the committee had come up with. No wonder bewilderment, even discouragement seeped in. Why hadn't they grabbed this combination of high tech and cloning?

They perked up; under questioning it became clear that the armadillo camel existed mainly in the inflamed skull of the general. Indeed, certain tics and quirks of manner, tendencies toward loose spit and shouting, nursed the suspicion that the committee had been had. The "expert" was in fact a patient from a military psychiatric hospital. He was oozed out; they drew a long, long sigh of relief.

But this is what they were exposed to, day after day; the bizarre, the cantankerous, the bigoted, the power boys who looked down on them, the religious fanatics groveling and groaning away.

The paperwork fell and fell an endless blank snow storm. Still they hung in. They studied and listened and debated and fretted. The experts had left town, a deadline was marching closer. Quality Control was also getting restive, the memos grew vituperative. What to do?

"Look," said the chairman, "Let's not lose our heads here. We've taken this thing seriously, done our work, given equal time to every wacko and weirdo in town. Let's call it quits for now and take the day off. Tomorrow everyone comes in with just one camel part, on paper, in your head, big, small, foolish, on target, whatever. Back to square one, so to speak.

"And just keep in mind, in spite of all the foolishness we've had to listen to, the thing is really quite simple. A camel is a camel is a camel." He closed his eyes, "Now let's pray together."

They bowed heads; his voice took on a tone befitting the occasion, solemn, basso. "O thou Who createst all . . . grant us at length . . ."

It worked like a charm—the prayer and a good night's sleep.

Came the morrow. Up and down the table went the word, bright, confident, flat, and final. It was like ten world-class contenders bending over the same jigsaw puzzle, this one, that one, near, far; every corner and angle falling in place; hump, foot pads, rubbery lips, disdainful eye, storage tanks, low literacy, bad temper.

They sat back, exultant. There it was, laid out; the very first camel of all. Seated on a hump behind the huge contemptuous half-closed eyes, rubbery smile—there they were, swaying on the great high hump: memsahib, Saharas, burnooses, palm trees, oases . . .

Here it came. You could hear it off stage, as though a rubbery horn were sounding the triumphant approach, nearer and nearer, the flatulent one, the arrival of the Very First Lesser Evil.

Latter Day Prison Poems
1) My Brother's Battered Bible, Carried into Prison Repeatedly

That book
livid with thumb prints,
   underscorings, lashes—
I see you carry it
into the cave of storms, past the storms.
I see you underscore
like the score of music
all that travail
that furious unexplained joy.

A book! the guards
shake it out for contraband—
the apostles wail, the women
breathe deep as Cumaean sibyls,
Herod screams like a souped up record.

They toss it back, harmless.
Now, seated on a cell bunk
you play the pages slowly, slowly
a lifeline humming with the song
of the jeweled fish, all but taken.

2) Prisoners in Transit

They took the prisoners, willy-nilly
on death's own outing
shod like dray horses
jump suits   pied like mardi gras

& curses & groans & ten pound shoes
& starts & stops
at every
station of the cross
across Wm Penn's
Sylvania

'Here's where that first trouble-
shooter started his last mile,' the guard yelled
    through his bull horn mouth—

'& here he did a phony fall—
gaining time was all
'& here it was
he rained like a red cloud
& here
we build his everloving ass
an everlasting memorial—

'this mile square Christian tomb
& closed the book

'You may all
come down now
take a 3 to 10 year
close look.'

3) *Poverty*

A prisoner is very poor—
1 face, 2 arms, 2 hands, 1 nose, 1 mouth
also 3 walls
1 ceiling
10 or 12 iron bars—
then if lucky
1 tree
making it, making it
in hell's dry season

I almost forgot—
no legs!
contraband! seized!
they stand stock still
in the warden's closet.
There like buried eyes
they await the world.

4) *Zip Code*

The precious info—
your whereabouts in the maze—
'Camphill Prison, Pa.' I memorize it
down to the absurd
talisman 1 7 0 1 1

Open Sesame!
the tomb shudders
a crack opens,
this wafer of life
slips through.

5) *A Few Gifts for the Prisoner*

The sea, a bearded mime
mimicking lambs and lions

The sun
betokening variety and
crystalline steadfastness.

Then one or two gestures of children
seizing, tossing, meandering—
like the prisoners, making
much of little.

Then an episode
of Luke's gospel; healing.
Let the prisoner bear that gift
onward, hands incorrupt, empty.

In and out of his cell
a flea circus trooping
too small for the guards' gimlet.

Let Christmas come around
for the prisoner alone—
cold, deprived, true.

And the angel
who succored Peter in chains—
enters
the prisoner's soul, whispers
Magisterially; Not yet, No
Not yet.

6) *Time*

To gain time
you must waste time
the 'waste'
an undercurrent—
passion, plethora

The smile, the daredevil eyes
More of same!
they bespeak
opposites, ironies,
repose, tears.

Gaining time, wasting time—
who shall do both?
a unitive fricative act
strikes sparks, blazes up,
reproves dire necessity,
burns away
irresponsibility.

Short of death's caught breath

I think of 'doing time.'
O my brother
when Christ steps
into time's
uncontrollable current
like a swimmer answering a cry—
He must do time—
those arms like wheels, that beat,
that nearing mercy

You
near. And He
mercy's sense and savior
grows, near.

7) *Penalties*

You in prison
I so to speak, at large
taste the penalty too—
half a world
half a loaf

like a two-legged dog
I saw once
body precariously balanced—
left front leg
right hind leg

tottering about, image
of half a soul
so to speak, alive
in the so called world—

the hunger, the
half a loaf called life

8) *Your Second Sight*

Walking by the sea
I put on
like glasses
on a squinting
shortsighted soul—

your second sight

and I see
washed ashore
the last hour of the world—

the murdered clock of Hiroshima.

           —from *Plowshares Poems*

Pax Christi—Spirit of Life Plowshares
(North Carolina, 1994)

1. The Court

Someone commands;
(the voice of the heart)
'Poetry even here!'

Obstacles; a brisk frisking,
descent among the dead,
worms fleeing into wormwood.
Portraits, faces
giving faces away, by Bosch.

Then the judge. A phiz like tallow's
sickly light,
night closing in. A Dogsberry,
don't tell him, he's
on leash, on loan to mercy.
'Time, twice time, half a time'—
dead fingers
conjugate apocalypse.

A gargoyle cries; All rise!
High, mighty, a soul in torment
turns to slime.

2. Judge

An epiphany—impeccable, impervious.
Is. From the beginning.
A triphammer for heart,
a piledriver look
laid the foundations.
Before him, nothing.

Foursquare, for judgment,
he laid out the world
you fondly thought was Christ's,
some gospel said so. No.

Seek no further
He's the great Why
guns are red eyed,
cops round bellied, the FBI
ax jawed, oak. Why
pay checks snow like manna
minions tread softly
juries quiver like catgut
under the punishing
suave bow of the maestro.

A baleful look,
and you'd better
hastily put on masks, sheep or goats,
baaing to right, butting to left.

And the walleyed totems
outstare you, big as billboards
wall to wall.
Primordial, stony, they turn
mere mortals to stone—

Always always
origins, the ace of starts—
judge begets judge,
judge clones judge
judge issues
from forehead of judge,
& naked, demure, subsuming
Venus hermaphrodite,
judge hoists his hosanna
steers a half shell ashore—

O you could talk
autonomy, dignity
till the gavel struck winter
and the words winged south—
but he holds court
tight as a lockup
tighter than lockdown

and the sheep
baptised in the blood
of a stillborn lamb,
and pneumatic as blimps
beatific ascend

and presto! the guillotine
speedy as centipedes
snicks & snees
goats to their knees.

3. The Verdict

The first day, my brother stood.
Sun shed dark
and leonine stood beside.

The second, I followed, somewhat.
The third to week's end
I leave to you to know.

Leave it to him,
his dignity, care, cue and—crime.
Something seen, said, done. Lips moving
as though under water;
words himalayan,
air thin, hardy
birds faint and fall.

Let's sit here and wait—
all we may, for the end.
Obey the prophets who say; wait
the benchwarmers, beggars.

Look; against all evidence, sun
shakes the dark once again.
Stands
to say so.

4. The Opposite

> Writing. I think; here's my hand
> grown older, no matter. Weaving this web
> like any spider, called words.
> Here, there ranging, hello brother.
> No matter who—my brother.

What's the opposite hard consonant
to web, web, airy weaving?
What's the wholly opposite, what's
all teeth, edgy, fricative,
so frontal and free
it breaks the metal cuffs of sheriffs,
gives wrists their hands, hands their
paintings, pianos, poems—

> hand to hand, the children,
> the dance of time yes, and
> no need of no, after years of no?

5. The Prisoner, the Cave

Ancients are writing with pencil stubs
scriptures in a cave.
What will be, what was
is, is, is in the cave.

Patience, a crystal, tells the time;
that and a cry, How long O Lord. That
and no reply. None,
and the outcry!

The parchment unrolls as they write—
a sky, a beyond,
a flying carpet, a throne
whence issue thunders; This Sayeth.

Love one another, they write. They love.

The cave is a pock on the moon.
The moon wastes and wanders,
a sea guarding its salt.

Unrolled one day, the scroll
will stutter, whisper, keen, thunder—
too low a pitch for humans,
lions plotting
the last day of the lamb;
a pitch too high, angels
rehearsing apocalypse.

6. The Gift

It's measureless
    Only the image, Son
  of the ineffable, takes its measure.

     Like this;
       joined hands, hardly seen
      (dusk to dark on the instant)
      behind bars, beyond all barring
      a beseeching; have mercy
        on the merciless!

     Like this, the measure;
    he casts ahead like a fly fisherman—
      Torment, truth. The take.

7. I Want You Free

Intemperate, temperate be damned.
     I want tempers riled, want
         vile matters resolved.
     I want you free.

      (No urge
   to wax metaphysical, metaphorical
like puppeteers in pulpits—
     'Of course you're free!')

      Justice?
   The word's a smear or sneer,
     the locks guttural as guards.
      No key turns, no tongued
freedom bell intoning 'free!'
Nothing. Bars adamant
     as justice held, withheld.

     Nothing?
     No.
     My love, the poem.

        —from *Plowshares Poems*

Lost and Found

There was once a man who couldn't for life or death, find his way in the world.

A dilemma. On the one hand, he was an irrepressible voyager. The world's map was a Baedeker—no, a very bible. He opened the map; it was transformed before his eyes. It was as though the creative Hand wielded a paintbrush, delicate, dipped in the hues of the first rainbow. Ah! Vermillion and ivory and cobalt and scarlet and verdigris and . . .

He knew it; he must walk into and become those hues, must, like a chameleon, welcome successive teguments begotten of sunset and desire!

So be it.

So it would not be. Let him but put foot to road and everything went awry. Shameless, treacherous maps were unfolded. Somewhere in the dark, they had turned north around to dread south. A compass he carried in his pocket veered wildly, and drawn forth proved a born spoiler. Go that way, its arrow said. Straight-faced. A liar.

In sum, our voyager, despite eager intent, got nowhere. Or rather and so to speak, he got somewhere called Wrongwhere. Jet planes, taxis, buses, ferries, subways, helicopters even—the world had wheels and wings, they purred at his door, they beat archangelically above his roof. Come with us, ride with us, fly away with us!

He went, he flew, he exulted—for a while. Picture him on arrival at a given destination. He is disgorged at an airport. From there, like the famed needle in the hay, his quest comes down to a small matter indeed; a matter of this corner turn left and that corner turn right, of street names and numbers, and the place he sought must—dammit—must be at hand. . . .

Alas, everything that seemed to work for everyone else, landing them exactly as a grain of wheat in its furrow, or a raindrop in the heart of a flower—hopeless!

It went like this, inevitably. He would arrive in some distant part. In a generic sense, he was There. Ah, but the Particular, that was the rub!

A merciful native, seeing him ogling and fretting over a map of the city, would pause, noting his dilemma. He would then trace a circle on the map (this is where you are); then another circle, near or far from the first, maybe overlapping (this is where you want to go.) Courteously, exactly, the distance, here to there, a line straight as an arrow. The directive angel would then wave good luck, and be off.

Things were indeed looking up. Our man starts out confidently, buoyed by simple kindness and a well marked map. He breathes easy, he feels like a balloon filled with preternatural gases, lighter than air, bound to earth by only the slightest of silken threads. Now, go for it! He has merely to cast off, float unerringly, from precise hither to exact yon.

Alas, the spirit is thin-skinned indeed; the most pneumatic mood invariably thumps down and down to earth. In his own city, on a given summer day, the heavens are rent by enormous sleek flying machines, shying from one another adroitly as a school of sharks.

And in their midst one afternoon, a great gas-bloated blimp was blinking its neon orbs, serving notice from on high as to the advantages of some indispensable amenity or other. It hovered there, to the wonderment of the earthbound. But not for long. Toward evening, stem to stern the pneumatic craft inexplicably shuddered, turned nose up precipitously. Down and down it fell, graceless as a deflated blowfish, to a tarred rooftop in our traveler's neighborhood. There was a moral here, he sensed, obscure but pointed.

Only give him and his quest a half hour. Then he begins to doubt. He turns the map about in his hand, trying to reproduce from where he stands, from where he faces, its mysterious legend: N., S., E., W.

Try as he might to correspond to these Euclidian points, from which (as he knows) radiates outward a rightly ordered universe: N., E., S., W . . .

One wrong turn begets another. Yet another and he is lost. His feet mire in the complexities of space. The streets are no longer peaceable or welcoming; they stand up, resentful as trodden harpies, mocking him.

As his mood darkens, so it seems, does the mood of the citizens around him.

To him (as perhaps to them) dawn had graced the earth with a kind of baptism. For an hour or two, time was redeemed from waste and bombast, from charlatanism and stacked cards. People wakened and walked abroad as though under a dewy waterfall, emerging white-robed into a new covenant.

The sun? It was as kind as a newly risen ancestor.

But in mounting it turned cruel; toward noon it transmogrified intto a furious laborer stoking a furnace. Humans, treading those fires, bowed low and were bound over, slaves of a slave.

Furnace, indentured slave, godling—the sun knew much, and refused all succor. It could point where east is, where west; it had been going and coming for millions of years. Excellent ancestor, speak!

O misleader!

What human skin, filled with whatever lightsome element, will mount and float and voyage for long, in face of those angry flares? Poof! And we are Icarus; we are downed.

✳

After many days and years, after multitudinous suns had risen and set and risen again, after expending like a Croesus of time, most of the days and nights granted a sojourner, after fretting and moiling and losing his way and his temper (and now and again as it seemed, his soul), at long last our peregrine did a simple thing—a thing that might have occurred to a wiser man than he—as the first thing of all to be done. He stopped in his tracks. To take stock.

To consult his soul.

How this or that renowned place, this enchanting vista, that lost city, or for that matter, this or that new film or newly minted book, the rage of the elite, the indispensable loot of all who breathed, the delicious jolt infused by spices, drugs, uppers or downers, the sting of quiescent lust—

He had walked the world, N., E., S., W., surveyed, weighed its wares and wonders. To a farthing, a pennyweight. Weighed them in scales against the featherweight of his own heart.

Which pan arose, lighter than what other? He thought to himself: possibly they are of vast import, these vistas, objects, beauties, sublime artifacts, and solaces. Possibly I should slacken a little the leash I have placed on appetite and its voracious maw.

Should I not leap to the teeming dug of the world? Should I not, like the vast majority of humans, make time, make hay, make—

Perhaps. But a difficulty persists.

In all these enterprises, efforts, obsessions, I find something strangely at odds—awry. I have never discovered, in the faces of hucksters and hawkers and possessors—never discovered evidence of joy.

Or if so, if now and again in the obscene millennial auctioning of creation, there appeared a standout winner, a wild card—the smile, the spoor—bearing his sack of piracies . . .

The stench of a shroud, the painted grin on a corpse!

✳

Such were the reflections of our gyrovague, as he stood before a museum in a city far distant from his own. The rose red city of desire! Half as old as time, painted on the aforesaid map by the aforesaid Hand.

He arrived with the velocity and baffling accuracy of a bullet.

Nonetheless, his old nemesis shadowed him. The closer he came to the quest, standing serene and noble in his mind, the more it took on the airy semblance of a mirage.

A wretched prelude. For hours he plodded along and missed his way and sought what help he could. And ever so slowly the city of light darkened. It grew positively stygian; it became in his mind a pit of vagrants and distempered snarlers. It was as though his geographic ineptitude had become pandemic; a series of locals responded to his inquiries with diabolic inaccuracy.

Calm down, calm down.

Success being as inexplicable as catastrophe, his long trek finally shortened, he trod at last the street of his dream. The great museum stood before him, storehouse and restorer, a shrine with its healing unguents.

With a pang, he entered the noble premises.

After many hours of peering, wandering, note taking, his eyeballs seared with the radiant plunder of the dead, he paused in a shadowy corner to reflect. Here, he said to himself, privileged I stand among the kings, robed in linen and crowned with gold. Kings who subdued their enemies like a flail from Gehenna, then handed the flail on to imperial sons of sons, who likewise would scatter the enemy like chaff to the winds. Winnowing the wheat of the world, lo! They gathered such plunder as is piled here.

And then? These mandarins, one after another, generation upon generation—to the vanity and despair and mournful flutes of their votaries—went down to the grave.

And behold. In this vast condominium of death I have peered into every face. And each, whether crowned with gold or molded in clay, is scarred with a look of cruelty, vexation, cynicism, greed.

Where in this theophany, this vaulting lust for immortality, will a seeker such as I come upon a face, like a torch beating its way through darkness, wreathed in a smile of joy?

And what am I to conclude? That their passionate urge (for immortality, for gold, for slaves, for a fond blessing, for mercy in a time of judgment)—that such desires seduced them from the true way?

Then and there, our traveler took resolve.

He would rejoice in his appointed fate, chancy and absurd as it was, the dizzy buffoonery of a blindfolded child spun about in the world, N., E., S., W.

He would refuse to renounce this game, his own, though it was bereft, beyond doubt, of good sense and logic. A way lost in a thicket or heavily trodden, rarely straight as a plumb line, often tangled beyond recognition.

Foolish, foolish!

He never forgot the joy of that moment.

He had looked the great kings in the eye; they were hooded and blind as stones of the road.

Burdened with his undoubted mortality, its panic and ineptitude and choler, he saw them, through and through. And they saw nothing.

He breathed deeply. And spoke, whether to them or to his own soul, in mockery or benediction, who could know?

"I travel the world beneath a banner. It is painted and lettered by no mortal Hand. Its legend. Arrived."

The Verdict

Everything before was a great lie.
Illusion, distemper, the judge's eye
Negro and Jew for rigorists,
spontaneous vengeance. The children die
singing in the furnace. They say in hell
heaven is a great lie.

                    Years, years ago
my mother moves in youth. In her
I move too, to birth, to youth, to this.
The judge's *toc toc* is time's steel hand
summoning; *come priest from the priest hole. Risk!*
Everything else
is a great lie. Four walls, home, love, youth
truth untried, all, all is a great lie.
The truth the judge shuts in his two eyes.
Come Jesuit, the university cannot
no nor the universe, nor vatic Jesus
imagine. Imagine! Everything before
was a great lie.

                 Philip, your freedom
stature, simplicity, the ghetto where the children
malinger, die—

                Judge Thomsen
strike, strike with a hot hammer
the hour, the truth. The truth has birth
all former truth must die. Everything
before; all faith and hope, and love itself
was a great lie.

               —from *Trial Poems*

The Wager

Three to one, absolutely a final offer, said the young one. A face like a whippet's, eyes in the back of his head.

The old one sat there, withdrawn, morose even. For more time than mortal calculation allowed, he'd worn that look. The classic elder, profile, chin on high—a wisdom beyond the usual, beyond the sum total of his counselors. Certainly beyond the machinations of enemies.

He was there; simple as that. There and in charge, and all's well with the world.

That it should come to this! In a sense, old man Olympus was stuck. Agreeing to the interview in the first place. Against all counsel.

In sum: you want the truth unvarnished; here it comes. You're sadly out of synch.

They drummed it at him, experts, old hands, economists, planners, lawyers. They wore crosses on gold chains, emblems of a brotherhood older than the Masons, tighter than the Maltese Knights.

His eyes rested on distances, long static vistas, as old as the hills. Theirs were camera shutters, aim and click. Get the picture, file it, catalogue it, it'll be useful.

Two ways of looking at the job, they'd lift their shoulders. And his way (they rolled their eyes), God for sure, is not our way.

He ran things like a messy think tank, muck at the bottom, free spirits paddling around on the surface, mysterious shifts and currents in between.

Did their eyes rest on the same planet? You could hardly credit it. To them, life came down to the Big Race; you took your odds and lashed the nag to the finish. They worked him over. Look, you can't have it both ways. Sit down with that one, you'll compromise everything. How does a camel get into the tent? Nose first.

Perverse, the old man coddled his thought: *I'd rather have one in my tent pissing out than outside pissing in.* But he said nothing; clean speech was a big issue that year.

No advisers allowed. The two sat there, opposite each other. Incongruous. The old one a listener, marks of reflection scored on his face, short beard and long shrift. The other hard, handsome in a concealing way, beyond pardoning or needing pardon. Move things fast. A tight spring. Hands made for fists. Eyes that give nothing away.

He spread his hands. Simple. He was after the old man's job. Nothing personal, a business matter. He could read the old face, a relief map, all desert and arroyo. Or better, a campaign map scoured, fired at the edges, all defeat and retreat.

After a touch of persuasion, a friend in the tax office handed over the records: GNP, budget outlay. The place was teetering on default.

From a certain point of view, things were just right. A takeover.

Bold as a mug shot, he laid out the odds: "Three to one I could do a better job. Give me one year, I'll get things humming. If I don't, you've lost—what? You're back in."

He reached over, gave the old man a nudge on the arm. It was pure contempt. "Go on, you deserve a break. Go take a vacation."

"Trouble with me," the old man's finger tracing a skinny dollar sign on the table top, "I haven't known for years what the job is." All those bad moves. What hadn't he tried? With advice, God help us, more advice than Job endured.

"You're too unworldly," the whippet was saying, shaking his head knowingly.

So he went off and joined a circus, hired out, a roustabout. Up before dawn with the brawns; slogging through autumn mud, heaving on the ropes, pulling the big tent up and up until it was all but airborne. Eating on the run, sleeping under the carts. Rain, mire, cold.

At least he got to see the show: the show before the show, so to speak; seeing it all come to life. Like a slow motion explosion of color and light under the enormous tent of sky.

Then the knockdown. It was like stuffing whole seas and continents, their flora and fauna and humans, into an ark. He sweated and groaned, stashing the world away in the pre-dawn, a dark grin on his face.

Then, good Christ, there was that religious phase.

He set up a glass booth in the back of a Midtown church, boned up on gestalt theory and Jung, set up a sign: THE PRIEST WELCOMES YOU!

Word got around. Rules, commandments, canon law? No questions raised, no *examen* of conscience required, no sorrow, no catalogue of delicts, and no purpose of amendment.

It was all free-floating, he and a client treading water behind a glass wall. Amniotic fluid, fishy smiles. He sat there, face and shoes agleam, a dark silky fish. His clients (God forbid, not penitents) lined up outside, Saturday evening at the aquarium.

God, whoever he or she might be—ground of being, love, stroker, comforter—out of sight, out of mind. Ecstasy? Despair? Shaft of light? Swoons? Penance? Sorrow? Sin? God forbid!

He was as cold as a coffin nail. Secular, soothing, gaseous, relevant as hell.

That phase came—and went. No catastrophe, no sudden falling off of impenitents. They still lined up in long, aching, subdued queues, or chattering away, waiting to take their medicine like orphans on the dole, uppers, downers.

Something happened nonetheless. A current ran along the dark insolvent lines, a wrist flicked the whip stock. Into the glass box nausea came creeping.

What was he selling anyway, sanitized euphoric hype, talk show talk? Feelings *uber alles*, faith dismissed with a modish shrug.

It came down to: nothing much mattered. Were they healed, sick, alienated, frightened, deep in muck, floating in illusion—what was illness anyway? What was health?

The lines were longer than ever.

One day he pulled up stakes and walked away.

The feminine issue arose.

An age-old discontentedness: they pointed with anger to his male court, male advisers, symbols, language. And in charge of everything, an ancient super male. Suddenly the women were armed with rambunctious historical studies, yesterday's naiads transformed to furies.

Up Mount Olympus they trudged, arms linked, an ancient energy tapped. The placard they carried was furious: OLD MAN, CLIMB DOWN! They chanted and circled the palace, standing vigil there in the cold and dark.

His counselors were dumfounded, outraged. Outraged was the official word; dumfounded the real one. Their own wives and daughters and lovers stood there, arms linked on the ramparts.

Olympus, neither dumfounded nor outraged, carried on officially, sensibly. He met with a delegation of the vigilers, ordered coffee and had sandwiches sent in. Truth told he was delighted beyond telling, this mandarin of the third eye, undrained of the juices of drama. His stance was neutral: all the while he was secretly reveling in the turmoil, welcoming the crisis to his marrow bones. Waiting the moment.

He was hemmed in, he knew it. He was like an ancient, infinitely wise, curia-bound pope.

Captive? Not for long. He found a way out, or someone did. One midnight as the guard was changing and the women huddled in knots about their fires, Olympus vanished.

✴

Where, no matter. It was a change, not of costume or custom, but far from this or that sweaty expedient. He turned his existence over.

A moment of mad energy: an insight that split his forehead and rent a great cry from the guts. Reborn, transvested, transgendered, he emerged as an "other."

Was courted, married, bedded, a "first" for any god known to this earth.

First, everything was a first. Known to any and all as Olympia, she conceived and bore two luscious daughters. One of whom became in time the operator of a Danish massage parlor, catering ambiguously. The other: founder, owner, publisher, editor, and distributor of a women's monthly, geared to the newly vocal international coven of Eumenides, Amazons, Dianas, Eves, the apollarians and ecstatics, harridans and Harpies.

Early on, in unmistakable terms, each of the offspring announced a washing of hands, cleansed of the following items: first and last and worst of all, religion. Then, mother and family, hearth and home—that tumbled sack of ineptitude—and piety and making do. Done, kaput, finished.

Religion! Family! They raised outraged eyes to heaven. Each repeated her renunciation, perhaps more frequently than required, (s)he thought wearily, interspersed with oaths newly minted and liberated; to wit, never again shall I so much as set foot in the shadow of a benighted church. Likewise, never again, any least truck with funky priests and their folderol.

And as for your musty family tree, your bizarre codes of conduct, budgets and boxes . . .

Amid a genetic debacle, reduced in spirit, the parent was led to question her past. Especially what might be regarded (two shrill absentee banshees punishing her skull) as excesses of parental piety, small noses pushed in holy water so to speak. Ancient enthusiasms, despite all intentions to the contrary, bringing only a karmic swing of the pendulum, poles by turn arctic and torrid, voids, hatreds, dis-affections. . . .

Ah, patience. For cold comfort, she recalled the women at the ramparts.

And more to the point, the reconnoitering within the palace, the puzzled half-amused looks passed along, pharaoh to functionary. Patience, magic and method, the cathartic, the universal solvent. Let's all be patient, the power boys sang like tuning forks struck.

The bitter taste of that medicine lay on the Olympian tongue, doled out, a universal placebo, blood wantonly spilled, tears useless-ly shed, words wasted, blows struck on empty air.

Take it; swallow it, the poison that heals. Or so it was said.

She reversed herself and came back.

The next phase was, if anything, even more scandalous: denounced by his council as irresponsible, unwarranted. Let's have it on the record; not for a minute did we OK that latest fool move.

Prosit. The old Olympian, by no one's leave, vanished once more.

He transmogrified into a croupier in Las Vegas. Time passed, he advanced, much valued by the management. Steady eye and hand, clear, authoritative, calling the shots. Bets gentlemen, place your bets! Skillfully raking it in.

Only to discover, after some months, yet another debacle. The circle of light in which he labored like a demon of avarice was wired for sound, bugged, and mirrored. The dice loaded. The wheel off-center. In sum, a crooked combine. He was their patsy, and liable before the law.

It was the most humiliating bootless crime imaginable. Invaluable? Skilled? He was a mink in a hole, scouting for the bagman. And all the while deaf, dumb, blind, undercover.

He was hauled once more on the carpet. His cabinet sat around; leaking vindicated righteousness.

No loss, no win, he thought, the eternal puritan draw.

The news hit the media, some smart reporter with a chip on his shoulder; headlines disgrace. Around the table, eyes, furious, contemptuous, weighing and wanting.

He's slipping fast, we're going to have the law in here one of these days. One thing is sure; from now on he's got to be supervised.

Still, matters stopped short of consequence. The meeting broke up, anger sputtered out. One thing he could count on: at the summit, conscience was strictly optional equipment. He took to reading Nietzsche. Found his life analyzed there, under the acid pen of a madman obsessed with the bad news of the universe. Pass it on, pass it on!

There's only one rule, Olympus whispered to his raked soul. It's simple, self-engendered as hell's fires. Things always get worse.

Not a word to anyone. One night, toward dawn, after a particularly lacerating night, he fled once more.

Transplanted himself to Italy. There in a remote mountain village he took to himself, body and soul, fate and no future—an ass, mangy and morose. By name, Cimerosa.

Thus he tasted for the first time, the bitter gall of the animal kingdom. Lashes scourged his flanks; he tasted the sour reek of rot-ten fodder, the fevers and paralysis of age, the stench of existence, animal existence. His own shit matted on untended flanks, his ribs tattooed by the staves of the ruthless.

His only reprisal was a desolate blank eye, hooves that ambled along in a pace too slow for profit. Staggering under burdens, the road invariably uphill, he came close to giving up.

So he gave up. On a day like every other day, the tether of awful days and nights frayed and broken at last, he breathed with relief a last breath. And saw with detachment his carcass carted off to a knackery, for whatever scant *lire* hooves and hide might bring.

Thereupon he passed several months at a spa, recuperating.

He would waken each morning in a stupor of dread, as though once for all he'd cast aside a human mien, destined to live with donkey ears, scrawling an ass's diary, the life and death of a dumb beast. He would rush to a mirror, half expecting to find an asinine Caliban staring back.

He recovered at length and promised himself a reward.

For every blow of the knout, every curse laid on him—the Good Life! Power! A name among men!

He sat straight up in his lounge chair. No more doldrums, boredom, illness, disaffection, scandal of soul. Exorcized at last!

At long last, he exulted; this is it. New skin, new soul, bang! Fist against palm, broad gestures, dignified mien, pride of place.

And the décor: alligator pumps, discreet gold reading glasses, manicured hands, mahogany desk, advisers and aides bustling about, crowds, promises, promises.

Tigerish, withal discreet; within hours he found the right mode. A compassionate reformer, aching for the political fray! Caballero on the left, denouncer and moralizer on the right, chic, reserved, an edge of derring do, stern of demeanor, a demon for work. Mandate, only give me a mandate, my grateful oft-cheated fellow citizens! For I have a plan!

Three nights in succession, he dreamed. Walking in driven snow, scarcely a foot track, white on white, my strength is as the strength of ten, my heart is pure. He heard a voice descanting the verse as though decanting old wine, precious beyond price.

He trudged on, and stood at length before a bronze image. Himself: mounted, heroic, twice life size, true to soul.

He awakened; embrace the dream!

And he was of course elected—a formality. Was adored. Swore the oath of office before delirious crowds. Adulation at last!

His soul opened like a parched landscape to a first godlike rainfall. The cheers rained on him, a perfumed downpour.

And thereupon, renewed, newly prophetic, he swore the oath:

TO UNITE IN MY PERSON & POLITY, BOTH YIN AND YANG, COMMONWEAL & RIGOR OF LAW, LONG SUFFERANCE & SWIFT JUSTICE, CONTEMPLATION & OUTREACH, PURITY OF HEART & RISK OF REPUTE, LOVE OF THE UNDEFENDED & SERVICE OF THE POWERFUL

And so on and so on. He dreamed on successive nights, now the occupant of the majestic House of White. Dreamed: of himself, of course. He was borne along in a Napoleonic progress; honors after toil, frantic huzzahs soberly harvested.

Thus the first month in office passed. He, learning his trade—from scratch.

Truth told, (after the fact it can be told), truth at the time was eased, blurred, codified, coined anew. Newspeak? No. Truespeak.

Truth telling? He was surrounded by guardian spirits, skilled in the ploys of power, prompting and hinting: "No comment at this time," was the soft not yet the time of seasoning, so to speak, of presidential timber.

Thereupon held a first policy session in secret. As chairman, he opened for discussion with a view toward immediate resolution, the fate of several thousand foreign nationals, undocumented, washed up on domestic shores. Though they dwelt within the free and generous orbit intoned by the bronze Siren in the Harbor, still the decision to discuss their fate rendered their fate questionable.

The decision, need it be added, was his. Next item. With compliance of foreign heads of state, he struck down two Third World frontiers as obsolete. As well as three more, touching on domestic passion and ethnic feeling, firmly and for the first time by common agreement and benefit hereby drawn.

That same week, he hosted a lengthy, off the cuff, mutually reassuring session with several heads of international cartels; attended a meeting, without immediate issue, but marked by cordial extra-curricular stroking in outer lounges, of buyers and sellers of the latest models of military hardware; hosted a session of his domestic cabinet, in the course of which, in view of mounting criminal activity and public alarm, the domestic death penalty was widened. Also the spine of drug laws stiffened.

Each Sunday, of course, he attended worship in what was billed as "the church of his choice." He sat somewhat ill at ease, uncertain as to the nature of the deity invoked, but urged to the gesture by associates, ever sensitive to public expectation; in view also of the paucity of dominical news bites.

At this time too, shaken by the greatly altered character of his dreams, he undertook in strict confidence consultations with an analyst.

One dream, in minor detail differing, was alarmingly recurrent. Snow intermittently falling: grey, gritty, polluting. Also, the recurring bronze likeness of himself unaccountably seemed to melt before his eyes, to fall away, horse and man. And from the horse's under parts, a kind of fiery piss issued, dribbling, dissolving the entire fundament.

Then a procession passed, he speaking not a word. The crowds in attendance were eerily silent. His mount halted in his tracks. And without warning there sounded a great bray or scream; it was as though the majestic creature he rode stood there, shaking in fiery agony or shame beyond bearing. Then the dream ended.

To speak of the analyst, he was no random choice; he bore weight in the fortunes of his adopted nation. A quondam obscure refugee, an arrow sharpened in the forge of a renowned East Coast psychiatric institute. Impeccable credentials!

And providentially so to speak, along came a war. An arrow this expert proved to be, and bow and arm to match. His target: government. The euphemism, the oxymoron, the sheer Danai shower of power: "service."

Self-service, it appeared, the first law of a healthy mind. This portent devised an intricate system of brain bending, useful both in domestic political games and the broad sweep of overseas policy. In sum, he could be counted on. Indeed, hardheaded; and this in a landscape (so he came to believe, his contempt barely concealed) of bleeding software.

His stock in trade was a nice blend of the brutal and subtle, the myth that heals, and the tag that conceals. He traversed widely and restlessly about his sponsors' business, legitimating, deligitimating as the case required, clients charged with the prospering of distant colonies. He read them head to toe like a scroll, the large text, the invisible writing. Were they following instructions, in matters major and small? He twitched a leash, signaling yes or no to the home port. Heads fell or fortunes improved, as the case mandated.

At home, he was no less successful; straightening the spine so to speak, of political Humpty-Dumptys, grown vertiginous in high places.

Thus he shuttled about the world or received domestic clients. Purposeful, mad, efficient, doodling on yellow pads his version of the world according to himself, crossing out those to be eliminated, naming those to be puffed.

One day a different patient at the door, a crestfallen glory. And was Herr Doktor, the prime brain of the century, to play minion to a dubious marvel?

The wilting president sat there. Doktor was by no means impressed. In his mouth there reposed for the moment, an old fashioned leather strap of a tongue. It could grow snappish, distempered.

The hour proceeded, accelerated, braked. He led our leader along the slender high wire of surmise, fantasy, fear. All those infesting second thoughts; tell us about them.

The voice of his client droned on like a metronome. The healer of spirits grew impatient. A pencil rattled against his teeth. He interrupted. Second thoughts, very well. Now—some first thoughts? He primed the dry pump. The polls were solid, weren't they? Things moving along, the dollar sound, the military keeping an eye on the world? The citizens believed, did they not, that a firm hand rested on the throttle?

Shore him up, this tottering tower. Repeated sessions, the same tack.

Two months later to the day, our changeling gave it all up, in horror.

Id locking horns with superego, impossible, an impasse. Was he to perish in a moral wilderness? And if so, for what good, what gain?

He could die, he could walk away. He chose.

In consequence of which, in a pub in Midtown, there he sat. Face to face across the table with a slick number, the keys of the kingdom about to change hands. Car keys, house keys, office keys, desk keys. Also credit cards, driver's license. Finally, the red key, the hotline, the code.

Not a doubt clouded his mind, only a measure of grief. What he was losing: the known, the familiar, a universe! And yet, and yet, time to move out, move on. He sighed, his hands trembled as he gave over—the symbols died as they left his hands, he was handing the universe to a dumb apprentice, he was handing coffin nails to an executioner.

With the sweep of an arm the opposition took it all. The gleam, the hard smile, the two-gear conscience. The winner looked at his watch, drummed the table, and pushed back his chair.

"So long old timer, old two bit loser."

Georgetown Poems (3)
I Hope and Pray This Doesn't Happen to Me

When the poet recanted
they hacked off his fingers
and gave him a signet ring

The poet recanted.
They tore out his tongue
and crowned him their laureate

He was then required
to flay himself alive;
two houses of congress
applauded, they dressed him
in the Aztec cloak of immortals

The poet surrendered his soul
a bird of paradise
on a tray of silver held
in his two hands

His soul flew away;
the poet
by prior instruction
vanished where he stood.

—from *May All Creatures Live*

Georgetown Poems (4)
On Being Asked to Debate H. Kissinger

When I sat down
they said with relief,
He's sat down at last.
But I hadn't. I was off like a shot put
and over their walls.

When I grew silent they said,
We've convinced him at last.
But they hadn't. I beckoned my soul aside
Come! pick apples, feed on your vision.

Then I stopped breathing.
They said in relief,
We can breathe again in the world
and deceive with virtuous tongues
and kill with immaculate hands.

And they could, they could. Except
for these lines, those apples, that vision.

—from *May All Creatures Live*

Ironies

Ironies
draw the mind free of habitual
animal ease. Sough of tides in the heart,
massive and moony, is not our sound.

But hope and despair together
bring tears to face, are a human ground,
death mask and comic, such speech
as hero and commoner devise, makes sense

contrive our face. To expunge
either, is to cast snares for the
ghost a glancing heart makes
along a ground, and airy goes its way.

—from *The World for Wedding Ring*

A Mouse Named Max

Once there was a mouse named Max who bragged unseemly. If he could be believed, he was in possession of nine lives—to be exact, eight after the current one.

Max was pushed into this realm of fantasy quite abruptly. One day, accompanied by considerable fanfare, a mouse evangelist rolled into town. Hot of eye, sleek, dog-collared, silk-suited: O, he was a boyo!

Reputation preceded him in a blaze. According to Standard & Poors, this Reverend could sell chunks of green cheese on the moon.

The day he arrived, as though out of a conjurer's hat, leaflets appeared in the town square. The Reverend, so it said, would arrive fresh from a triumphant European tour, gingering up the Christianity of Rome, Geneva, and other hot spots of religious deviance.

He arrived amid a splendid cavalcade; his car was a vintage Mercedes, painted sky blue, with here and there a daub of immaculate cloud. That and a liveried chauffeur. The engine purred; the preacher sat enthroned, like a dusky cherub on a baroque ceiling, temporarily grounded.

Enveloping his chariot, a vast red banner, like a cummerbund on a putto, proclaimed: PRESENCE OF THE PROMISE AMONG YOU. THIS EVENING. 7:30 PROMPT. TOWN FAIRGROUNDS. COME GET YOURSELF SAVED ONCE FOR ALL!

Evening came, excitement was rife, and all roads led to the camp meeting. Rich and poor streamed in, tottering old Fords on their last legs, hunkered down covered wagons, Mafiosi Cadillacs with drawn curtains. Spotlights sliced the night sky; the media was on a feeding frenzy.

After an hour's trumpeting and drumming, the lights went down. Then a spotlight, shinnied about like God's own eye, seized on the reverend. He sauntered down the aisle, arms stretched wide to the adoring throngs, rings and bracelets dazzling the eye.

"Welcome, thrice welcome to ye who assemble, in despite of a godless time, in this godly place! Saved, yea ye shall be saved, all who seek salvation.

"Be comforted my people. Solemnly I tell you," he intoned, "there is a God above who takes in account every hair of your chin, every hapless pelt seized. Why even now, those mousers are lurkin' and smilin' out there in the dark. Where according to the good book shall be heard only wailing and gnashing of teeth."

His auditors swiveled about, fearful eyes turned to the encircling darkness. Were the believing throngs surrounded by a circle of hungry green eyes?

"Furthermore and to continue," he went on, his voice careening up and down the scale, from squeak to near roar, "I tell you solemnly, if in the paws and jaws of you know who—if ye lose this life—why ye shall gain another and a better! And yet another, yea, unto the ninth transmogrification!

"But be warned. That life after life, that great endless good time, nine times over, pelt and ear and tail all renewed, moon upon moon of cheese yer own—" his voice dropped to a conspiratorial wheeze— "I aver and swear to you, faithful an' true, this undoubted miracle is not for the common run or kind. No not a bit of it!

"Life beyond life is promised to none but the open hand an' the open pocket! The mouse prevailin' is the mouse prepayin'! Give an' it shall be given unto ye, pressed down an' flowing over!

"To get down to cases," he slapped one hand against another, the gold gleaming like the eye of a sunrise, "I need not inform anyone present, how near ruinous it is to plain, unlined pockets like mine, maintainin' this absolutely first-class evangelistic group, freely appearin' in your midst this night.

"Just look aroun', fresh from Europe! First of all your eyes rest upon . . . me, your servant an' reverend. Then these peerless li'l women singers, whose sweet voices would make the angels pause in mid-flight, all ears an' close to tears.

"Moreover,behind this here stage take my word, makeup artists, prompters, numerous PR men doublin' also as ushers, as you see in full dress. An' chauffeurs an' cooks an' I don't rightly know who else.

"Where in the world I ask you, do believing eyes rest on such wonders anymore?—elegance an expertise on all sides—an' all fer yer sake! In this godless world of cat eat mouse, an up-to-date electronic Presence of the Promise thus flourishin'!

"But to revert. The Nine Lives belong to those who hand over—nine fold!

"In such wise, blessed spirits proceed by grace up an' up the ladder of Jacob. To life after life after life, yea even unto the ninth rung of that-there crystal stair.

"Therefore an' likewise. Kindly cough up—an' ye shall rise up. Amen."

Concluding, the preacher vanished from the pulpit with a flash of gold and a flick of tail. An organ struck up the national anthem.

On the moment a corps of winsome female mice, attired in robes of gold and silver lamé, launched down the aisles like a flotilla of Cleopatras en banc. Each bore a collection basket in hand. They sang reedily as they came: "Come ye blessed, give, give, give and ye shall ever live, live, live."

Max paid up, everyone paid up. The containers speedily overflowed. Nine lives!

All minds were fired.

Friend Max returned home, his head in a whirl.

✳

Now about Max. A bachelor, confirmed. His dwelling, a burrow at the root of an apple tree in Farmer John's orchard. Ideal. But still, promise or no, nine lives or one, like every mouse in creation, Max was misfortunately trailed and shadowed. The troublemaker was a large mean-tempered angora cat named Ferdie—moody, wall-eyed, easily turned berserk, governed by a rampant persecution complex.

A terror by repute, Ferdie prowled and hunted by whim and moon phase. Most days though, he lay around like a frayed rug, snoozing and hanging out.   This uncertain terror was also seized at times with melancholic fits, mainly due to his inability to make mincemeat of Max.

For his part, the Christian mouse despised the cat intensely, and lost no chance to make sport of him.

On occasion, Ferdie came alarmingly close. Once or twice, he even managed to thrust a wet nose into the mouse doorway. The maddening whiff of mouse meat did little or nothing to relieve his feline frustration. So near and yet so far! Ferdie gnashed his teeth, his prey just beyond clutch.

Max, safe and sound in his lair, would jig about, mocking his persecutor mercilessly. "Of course I'm in here, you big idiot. O you're hungry I bet, you frickin' bully!

"Just look at yourself," the mouse squeaked, "Ten times my *avoirdupois*, and you can't lay a glove on me.

"Why don't you take on someone your own size?" Max launched a kick of his heel at Ferdie's nose, raked him with his tiny fingernails, hissed and hummed up close, "Catnip, shnatnip. Coward cat, 'fraidy cat!"

Ferdie withdrew in a frenzy.

Max for his part, grew cocksure. Nine lives, didn't the preacher say so? He had nine lives! Morning and night he dreamed and ruminated.

"Let's see," he muttered one day, stretched out on his futon, chain smoking. "Nine lives, eight to go. I'll be a city mouse then a country mouse then a doctor mouse then a lawyer mouse then a tycoon mouse then"—he gave a foolish leer and slapped his knee. "Then a Don Juan mouse!"

Now it must be admitted that our friend was a wicked one for the ladies. From time to time, too frequently for anyone's good, he held an open house for a gaggle of females; a number of them, alas, of dubious repute. Time after time the gatherings got shamelessly out of hand. Nightlong there was roistering and carousing and loud rock music—live—issuing from drums and snarling guitars. Max would wander hither and yon among his guests, showing off his meager biceps. "Lookit those muscles, ladies! Ten to one," he cried, "I give you ten to one I outlive that ol' polecat Ferdie! No, fifteen to one!"

The ladies squealed and applauded.

But as good children know, such arrogance as is here reported cannot long prevail. Max and his demesne, to put matters shortly, went by degrees to . . . sleaze. The fire died in the hearth, dishes lay unwashed in the sink, garbage piled up, and the roof sprang a leak.

Max took to wandering around the slovenly premises, humming a foolish song of his own composition, "Polecat Sniff, Ferdie Whine, Nine Good Lives Shall Yet Be Mine."

Turn and turn about, Max drifted out of this world. In one fantasy, he, a renowned surgeon, oversaw the dissection of Ferdie and hung his taxidermied head on the wall for a trophy.

In another fantasy near to dementia, he stood in court, defending a revolutionary group known as the Weathermice.

And yet again—but some of his meanderings are too gross for tender ears.

In time, I regret to report, the mouse also became—a souse. It happened thus. There stood concealed in a grove not far from Farmer John's house, a mysterious homemade contraption consisting of a copper pot and piping, a fire grate, and an oaken cask. Night and day around the huffer fires were stoked. A mysterious liquid bubbled and burped away, passing drop by drop through pipes into the barrel.

The sound was both satisfactory and mysterious, like the gurgling of a satiated gut after a good meal.

Meandering about one night, Max heard it. His ears went up. Idle as usual and possessed of a spirit fantastic and frolicking, Max tiptoed into the garden and approached the still.

He put his lip to the drip at the tip of an oaken cask. A fateful moment! Farmer John's barrel was reeking of—moonshine! A liquid, I need not add, altogether foreign to the dietary habits of mice.

And moreover and worst of all, unsanctioned by law.

Max licked his chops. His head bobbed, up and down, up and down to the spigot, again and again. His eyes rolled glassily under the moon.

Time passed. Let it be confessed: Max became a fervent toper. By night and day, a trespasser on dangerous ground, Max beat a path to the leaky barrel.

His illusions became ever more fiery and vivid. He took to weaving about his quarters, posing in front of the mirror, pushing out his chest.

"Less see," he'd mutter, "lawyer mouse, doctor mouse, Don Juan mouse! Then what?" His eyes rotated foolishly.

"I've got it, Super Mouse! I'll show that blasted cat! Put up your dukes, scaredie cat! You've met your match an' then some!" He staggered around the room, weaving, dodging like a punch-drunk boxer. And nothing in sight but his own skinny shadow. Finally he threw the door open and, full tilt, made for Farmer John's barrel and his ration of sundown grog.

He put lip to tip.

Then POW! WHAMMO! Out of nowhere, cleaving the sky like a last day, down it came: a paw like a blasting blunderbuss.

Alas and alack, requiescat mus.

The moral of our tale?

A grain of salt. Preachers, like many among us, from time to time, and in prospect of beneficial greenery, spin tall tales indeed. Ruin may well follow, of mice and men.

Hymn to the New Humanity
(Nicaragua, El Salvador, and the U.S. June, 1984)

The guns are common as stacked firewood, and as cheap.
They are common as walking sticks carried by the aged and infirm.
There is a gun for every contra who carries a gun.
There are toy guns for infants and flowery guns for little girls.
To the delight of children, there are clown guns that go
!popopop!—and wouldn't harm
   an insect.
There are chocolate guns for Easter; guns that spout water and guns
that sprout a parasol
   for rainy days.
The guns of course have eyes. The guns of the Guardia Civil have ears.
   And there are merchant guns that smell a dollar, like a miser's nose
in a sirocco of
   money.
And statesmen's guns, equipped with silencers, sheathed like their
owners in raw silk, a
   spiffy outfit.

There is a rare gun, a gun of dark rumor. The ultimate gun, the gun
named god. Like
   god, it has never been seen; in virtue of the invisibility, it must be
believed in.
Somewhere, no one knows where, whether on land or sea or in the
air, this gun is
   sequestered, stroked, nourished by the hands of servitors.
Like the queen bee of hell, it waxes in the dark; fed on morsels of
children, boiled eyes
   and pickled ears. It is indifferently a carnivore, a florivore, a fauni-
vore.

This is a metaphysical gun. It renders all other guns, together with their makers and
  users, redundant.
It is aimed at the heart of history, the secret wellsprings of life.

Innocent as the three famous monkeys, guns see no evil, speak no evil.
Guns believe in guns, guns hope in guns, guns adore guns. In the new dispensation, these
  are honored a theological virtues.
There are loving marital guns. They vow fidelity, each to the other, at the altar of
  revolution. Thereupon they are blessed by clerical guns in white surplices.
Also guns are laid on the table at Mass, next to the bread and wine; then they are said to
  be consecrated guns.
There are guns held by sheep and guns held by goats. To the former Christ says: Come
  ye blessed. To the others: Depart from me. Or so it is said.
In El Salvador, the guardia peer out from behind the smoked windows of vans, like
  Mississippi sheriffs behind their shades; the look of a leveled gun.
In Nicaragua, the guns have learned to smile; like cornucopias of metal, they whisper
  promises; Dear children, trust us; from our barrels pour the ABC's, medicines, a blessed
  life. Trust us, stroke us, vote for us. In our dark void is concealed all your future.
It has proved embarrassing on occasion that the Christian documents are recusant on this
  matter of guns. Exegetes, artists, poets, intellectuals have been moved in consequence,

to create as it were, a contrary hypothesis. The empty-handed
Christ, they declare,
   "would have," "must have," "might have"
carried a gun. Or at the least, he favored their legitimate use; just
guns for just causes.
In the older iconography, the hands of Christ are by no means
empty. They bear the
   bounteous fruit of a storied imagination: shepherd's staff, teacher's
scroll, a lamb or
   two, wheat, chalice. Now these sublime and simple things are lifted
from his hands.
   Even that bloody heart, livid as a skinned plum, to which his index
pointed as a very
   sigillum of love—it is torn from his side.
We have in fact imagined a better way of imagining him than he
was capable of.
What has occurred is roughly this. There came a time when it was
no longer possible to
   venerate the older symbols of the holy and human. Our species
evolved, in accord with
   exigencies of time and place.
A new human emerged from the tired womb of tradition; a tradition which here and
   there, through service of lip and heart, had preached a cult of—
gunlessness.
A gauche ideology indeed! On its behalf, believers failed to coin a
usable term.
   Nonviolence? It was a clumsy transliteration. They were gunless,
that is all.
Our own times signaled a breakthrough. Guns were no longer mere
instruments of bleak
   choice. They were now simply a matter of wholeness, morphology.
To this point, to be
   born gunless corresponded, in the ethical sphere, to a mishap in
nature; an armless or

legless or sightless being; one lacking in a substantial component of the human.

Thus, to bring a long matter around, a fresh light is cast on a very old subject.

Meantime, it must be admitted that a few recalcitrant priests and their sequaces spurned

the light. In public places they intemperately cried out the old credo to their gunless

god. They were dealt with, summarily.

Our genetic leap postulated a new ikon. The older images had died with their god. They

were best buried, once for all.

In this matter we were relentless: new humans, a new god.

Our theology produced a generation, not of iconoclasts, but of inspired entrepreneurs. We now possess, in plaza and shadowy corners, in discourse and dance, the Christ we

have come so richly to deserve.

—from *Hymn to the New Humanity*

The Loser

There was a dead man. A loser of note. Of whom, more presently.

Call him Omnis, a family affair.

I summon the life he lived. Faces, a house, a yard and garden; then the subtler things, likes and dislikes turn and turn about; food and drink and people—and a task.

Give him a task and all sorts of things clarify; the lines on his phiz, the grasp of his hand, the look in the eyes.

Unmarried. Two sisters, also unmarried. At the very least, not one of the three would die in the subversive or boring or drab company of—himself, herself.

Two sisters, a brother, their lives. Church, state, war, peace, plenty, penury—also neighborhood, friends socializing, small talk of summer nights—these care for themselves; they recede, dimming into a background, a haze of time past.

There's a slight companionable hum in the background of his story; one remembers a good family, ups and downs. And now and then, a shouting match. Thus it goes.

Perhaps at length we have conjured him, the makings of a life, a reputable fiction, something in itself approaching the sublime. Tread softly.

Toward the ending of the story, interest mounts.

Illness has taken him in hand, a hand hitting hard; his life is slipping away. Call him loser in a general sense, the sense that applies to all.

Death.

But our friend is also a loser in a personal sense. A special loss is looming. It's as though he must endure what the bible calls "the second death." A friendship is also failing him. To know the loss of such a friend, what that means, the equivalent death, you must have known the best of it, the gift that comes, if one is lucky, once or twice in a lifetime.

Omnis had known, or thought he had known, the best of the gift. In his illness, in fever and chill and gnawing weakness, he conjured the image of his friend, and was comforted. In dreams his friend stood at bedside. Blessed by this presence, he, Omnis, was content beyond all merit.

Must he then die? Very well! Now and again he intoned or shouted this aloud, "Very well then," in a kind of delirium. And the phrase held no hint of despair or rancor. For his friend stood there.

But the friend was not there. And in consequence, as we relate, Omnis is a loser in this awful sense. Death approached. And the friend kept his distance. (The thought crossed the mind of the sisters too in their wearying vigil. If the friend entered and stood there, his healing hands, his stalwart tenderness, would not death be pushed back?)

The sisters: we'll send a message. "Your friend is ill."

Omnis failing, dying, subdued turmoil around him, the play of memories, regrets, sweetness, and the grief that issues in bitter tears.

One day, going, going, he was barely breathing. Around the bed the grieving sisters joined hands.

Weeping, scarcely audible.

A grief so particular, grief that like a tracing finger in the dark, bringing the face of a lover ever so lightly into being.

By touch, by blind touch.

And at the center of it all (as though indifferent to all, but surely not so), barely breathing, this deathly figure, this marmoreal stillness.

A face once likened to spring weather, mobile and changeful. Now a sculpture is cast. Shortly it will cool into final form. He breathes shallowly, with heart-wrenching effort. The sisters keep watch, involuntarily breathing in rhythm with him, alert to the pain, the indrawn effort. As though, as though, they would draw breath for him.

To be at his side is their passion. This concentration, this living for sake of, breathing for sake of—it is hardly conscious—beyond words, intense and solitary.

Through the night, the eyes of the sisters rest on the dying man. They are withdrawn from this world. They draw for another the breath of love, beautifully, harmoniously, hardly conscious.

The two, and a few friends, hover there through the night. An exhausted dawn arises. And in the watchers dwells a communality of grief and purpose.

The night has been a black bolt of veiling, winding them and him in one swath of loss. Yet and yet. They fondly think (a fiction of the heart), that through them he has survived another night!

Dawn comes, exhaustion takes them.

Each of the vigil sitters was living, in a sense, a double life; that concentration, terrible to behold, on the barely living. And one ear toward the door, a knock awaited all the night long.

It never came.

Dawn came. And the sick man was slipping away.

Why did the friend not come? Would not a friend have found occasion and hour, would not the heart of friendship have impelled him to their side, at whatever cost?

Still they awaited, in a kind of stupor of hope, a failing hope. Awaiting the healer, the friend of strange powers.

Then doubts, creeping over them like a dawn chill. And if, and if only—an unfinished sentence in the mind. That long, long wait and no issue.

That day the brother died.

The sisters are on their knees now, around the bed, in the imme-morial gesture that says, it's all over, nothing left but a prayer. The sad rites begin—the tears, the washing and clothing of the corpse, the merciful distractions.

And that ache, the question unresolved. Why, again why? Could he not have come, their urgent message received ("your friend is ill"), to offer in a dark time a measure of relief?

Does not love urge it, the setting aside of lesser affairs?

The friend is dead. And the healer is . . . absent. Rather, in that strange phrase, he has absented himself. By choice, by inadvertence, by carelessness?

And then, this. All hope vanished, hope against hope. And tardy and contrary to expectation, into the house of death arrives the healer. He enters without a word and stands above the corpse of his friend.

The body laid there, a kind of dumb reproof.

And the words of the mourners, greeting, reproof, a wisp, a hint of—something. If you had been here . . . Which is to say, if you had come in time . . . Or, Why did you not come, while we still hoped?

Unspoken, but strong in the mind; resentment too, even a sense of betrayal.

Why are you here, too late, too late? Would it not be better, if other matters governed you, held you away, to underscore by remaining afar, the death in this house? The death, too, of friendship?

And he answers. He challenges their questioning, the reproof in their eyes. He conveys a far different sense of absence. His sense is terrifying; it is like a stone in the mouth of a cave, impenetrably blocking reason. "You call it hope betrayed. But I am powerless, until what you call "hope" is gone."

This godlike one! An edge of cruelty? What he inflicts on those he loves.

As for the dead man, he must be accounted, in the strict sense, even in death, a witness, an actor in the drama.

In death he is of interest only to a few, his sisters, a small circle of friends. Of no interest to the powerful or to the unborn (to ourselves), this obscure life, obscure death. Of interest only to those who love him, who could not save him, even under an urgent lost rubric, a panicked message gone on the wind.

If that were all, then that were all—as is said of death, a sentiment commonly accepted. Or fiercely resisted—what difference?

But that, we are told, was not all. There occurred a wild eruption in the course of nature, an event of note, even of notoriety. A death not, finally, banal.

Over this one, dead as the coin on his eyes, no ceremony would plead, "requiescat in pace." Nothing of this. Over him would play the lightning of divine irony. An irony that refused to succor him while living, and in death, banished peace from his bones.

Choose it or not, the dead man will live; this is the decree. He would live (with no choice in the matter), as icon of the living God. A living proof, as they say.

He is snatched from obscurity and decay. A word called final is denied finality. He is to show in death that death shall have no dominion.

A body snatching power, as told. A power that made of the dead the formerly dead. In plain fact, the "raising from the dead" hardly encompasses the event; call it rather the transfiguration of the dead.

I leave to others details of the outcome, the coming alive of the dead. Leave it to others to tell the wiles of that healer, who neglected a lesser miracle for sake of a greater. Who allowed a vast grief its hour, for sake of an incomparable relief and joy—and terror.

The grief turned suddenly to wild joy. Or so it is said.

But is grief so easily turned on its head, without danger to sense and sanity itself?

Must grief not be traversed like a spiral, slowly, from a tight center to a larger relief—scarcely to be called joy? And must not this dark passage be granted time, months, years?

In a moment, the grief of the mourners was turned to an onset of joy. So it was told. The healer commanded, the dead arose.

But still, like a dragging shroud, a suspicion clings to the scene.

Had the risen one something to tell? Could it ever be told? If so, could they bear to hear it?

And who of the household would meet in equanimity of spirit, the glance of the formerly dead, that unfathomable look? Was there comfort afterward in that house, its visitant returned from God knew where?

Let us pray.

Merciful one, succor us from the tyranny of a second death, or the terror of a second life. Grant us to die in due time, in a modicum of peace. Lead us to whatever world awaits. And in whatever judgment, have mercy.

And may we live in peace and die in due course, free of wonders and visitations beyond mortal bearing.

Amen.

The Newstand

In cold November
the old man stood
all day
in a flimsy canvas box,
struts, patches;
        a lung, a world
billowing with big portentous names.
The stone man stood;
        drumming like a god
wars, death,
        time's bloodletting and getting.

At sundown
        the world came apart,
a shack of cloth and board
        roped, hefted.
Last, rolled up his pages;
        the leonine faces
snuffed without cry,
        dead as day.

—from *No One Walks Waters*

Masks

"Yes. To be sure. Skin's the trade," he would say, face close to yours, serious as the grave.

"Or more exactly—and surely we can trust each another—masks."

A bleak cranny he inhabited, a lame excuse for a shop. We're in Dickens's London, you'd think, or the back streets of Conan Doyle. Summon a waste of fog, clattering hooves and black draped carriages, dastardly deeds afoot, the decor of Victoria's last lumpish days.

How wrong you'd be. We're in New York City, time—present.

Look sharp, such a place still exists, in Chelsea or the East Village; or one of those cul de sacs that seemed two centuries ago inexplicably to rise from nether regions long before the east west, north south grid made the city a case study of Yankee logic gone haywire.

Well, as to our shopkeeper. Skins, masks did he say? No, the words are a cover. What matters came to were—faces. And if you wanted the whole truth—souls. But the whole truth, or something approaching it, waited on an outcome.

Imagine this. Through someone or other you'd heard of him and ventured in, a heavy matter on your mind. You wanted a stranger to tell it to, someone anonymous.

Touché. You had it in him, someone, and no one, a colorless bundle of duds hung on a skinny frame.

Were you sizing him up?

No time lost, he was sizing you up. And then a grin, coming and going like a tic in his skull. He had you.

The advantage. He had you in the dry palm of his hand. Then he was grinding away at you with his thumb. It was like sandpaper against skin. And you stood there and took it, that look of his, turning like a gimlet in your skull, boring in to where the fear lay, and the dread.

"At your service." He bowed, crooked his elbows, then swept his wiry arms wide. "What could I do for you?"

There were rules of course. His goods and services were, shall we say, perishable. They were designed for one occasion—only and strictly. He was adamant on that. No playing permanent roles, no fooling around with dark emblems, his creation.

Once he accepted you, things started to move. A spider hurrying, hither and yon, up, down the web. "Let's see, let's see. Step over here to the light." He ran two hands up and down your face. A touch here, a pressure there, those eyes at the tip of his fingers.

The hands dropped. "Come back a week Friday; it'll be ready."

One after another they came, hapless votaries to a dark shrine. He heard them out—the hangdog pretension, the shame and sorry pride—his head to one side, nodding away like a metronome, lips pursed in spurious simpatico.

The types who sought him out! A lover, wanting time off from the onerous burdens of love. No questions asked. Oh, he did, he understood, winking and grinning like a gargoyle come alive. Of course, of course, let's face it, facts of life, no harm, a bit of a fling . . .

Another, a face like a botched lie; untruth a stigma on the mouth. Money, big money, almost in his grasp, the deal of a lifetime.

But his face, to put the matter shortly, got in the way.

No problem. Our skin man would smooth out those telling ambiguous lines; induce around the eyes a few responsible crows' feet. Rehab the mouth—a touch of innocence.

There came a priest, uneasy in his black straitjacket, a funeral ritual to be gone through. But the mirror was not reassuring. How correct that sardonic worldly eye? How make the message viable: tears, only believe, resurrection and life, etc., etc.?

"Tinkling cymbal," the priest had to read it straight-faced from the book; "Empty brass . . ." Had to mean it—or look as though he did.

"But the greatest of these is love . . ."

The old man eyed him. "Yes. We shall try."

Deferential as the devil himself. And all the while sizing him up, sizing him down. "We shall try."

Always that plural, as though somewhere in the back of the shop, subalterns lurked, shadowy hired hands. Nothing, in sum, he (or they) wouldn't take on; lives, follies, contumely, ruin, crime. Nothing he couldn't patch up for an hour or two, an evening's sweet cheat.

He heard them out, the whine of born losers, the boasting of high rollers. They departed. He spat to the floor.

Enter a client, a final fitting.

All goes well. The new face is pressed against the old, tight as a chamois glove upon a hand. It fits, it conceals, it deceives, and it offers smiles of a summer night. It can smile and be a villain. Or see, it makes a fist of a face; a publican calling in a bad debt.

"Perfect!" The old man stepped back, spread his hands.

They came and came—to pay up, to report success, to thank him. Relief, triumph, the illusion holding firm. They were like gleeful lost souls in an old wives' tale, reporting to the chief imp.

They turned and went. He was yawning behind his hand.

✵

He filled their dumb spaces with his moving lips, followed their chatter, eyes half closed. In them, illusion; in himself, mastery. He rendered them like fat on a hot stove—he stirred the pot, they boiled down, next to nothing.

A mere touch of the hand was like a mind reading a mind. He pressed against skull and throat, held for a moment. Then his hand moved gently along the line of cheek. He froze them—to their choices.

They went away, wearing a new emblem, faces sculpted of an impurity so pure it mirrored their souls.

He created—lives. Out of parts, discards, relics, ruins.

"Mask my corruption," they cried, "make me young, make me honest, Oh, for an hour!"

He delivered the goods, they ate his skills alive.

It was only a game, he told them, told himself. "*In principio creavit Deus.*" Was he not also an artist, was he not making a world? If reproach was due, let it fall on those who sought him out, who came cringing or bullying to his door.

The sages of this world, whatever their metaphysical leaning, are agreed on this image: a mysterious gavel rises and falls. The final look of creation is a court of law.

One day, the gavel fell. Someone, something—an intervention.

Always before the fitting, the final touch, mask to skin, don't move, a few moments, then—perfection. Here: he held a mirror up. Skill, timing—everything right.

But now, something else; things nearly right, not quite right. Did his hands rest a few seconds too long on the altered face, was the formula going awry? Too hard a pressure, impatience, a feather-weight of carelessness?

Something else? Something leaping back to his fingers—a message from nerve ends.

It was as though in that musty room the bottles and vials and drawers, the broken discarded masks, the dusty roots and herbs, the dried skins, the vials of glue, all the clutter of creation—as though these were coming alive, stirring in place, shifting, whispering.

And a stench, heretofore unnoticed.

It unnerved. Something was going awry. The clients couldn't nail it down, a stench that arose in the gloom, a miasma.

And that grin, off, on. And the contempt in his dead eyes.

Still, he ignored it, said nothing, an old necromancer viewing the world through a gimlet.   A hunter through a gun sight?

This followed: an ending of note. A morning, its memory seared like a brand. A policeman was routinely rattling latches and locks along his beat. He came to the premises of our wonder worker. Ordinarily at that hour, the place was bustling with life.

He rattled the latch. No light, no one coming and going. The door was unlocked.

Our minion of the law entered. Toward the rear of the shoddy box, as though shadows stood vigil, lay our merchant of megrims. Floored. Above and around, careless and uncared for, tools, hooks, eyes, sketches, knobs and drawers, dust and ashes, ears and noses, grins, frowns, wax, burners, threads, tapes, cracks and cobwebs, hollow places, secret drawers.

And on the floor amid the clutter, he, fallen. In the cave of his calling ungainly sprawled.

The policeman stood above, turned to stone. On the face of the dead man, a look that could freeze blood.

Let the medical report in no wise second the frenzied rumors that attend such an event. Another death in the city, all said a quotidian urban passage. Accidental or malicious or premeditated or . . .

But surely no whirlwind, no apocalypse.

To be exact; on the face of the Master of Masks lay the burning impress of two purposeful thumbs and forefingers, right hand on left side, left hand on right. The impress burning through the flesh, darkening the bone—a brand, a stigma.

Ownership, claim?

The police were reticent, as is their wont. Nevertheless, lucubration was set steaming in the common mind. What had occurred in that shop, at some unknown hour before dawn?

For the record, continued.

Item: the features of the departed, fixated as though in a marmoreal scream.

In any case, a vindication of sorts?

For the event of that day, as goes without saying, his victim clients were quite unprepared. Neither he nor they being, in the final instance, the aggrieved party.

Months, years have passed since our magician was summoned from this world. A subsequent history of his clients may be of interest.

Those who sought out his skills, and under his spell suffered injury of spirit, frozen in this or that mime, in a false self imposed—all, severally and singly, were gradually freed.

Winter passed, their smiles returned like northbound swallows. They resumed former lives, liaisons and losses, spouses, hostilities, poses, defiances, dead losses, surrenders.

In sum, they appeared neither better nor worse than before. At ease upon the pavement, specious and swaggering at the familial hearth. Secure in their fronts and faces, they drew breath, each his own dog, slave, victim, shadow, semblance.

Alive, alive! Once they were all but floored by dread and deception; now they blinked like lizards and turned to the warming sun.

Thus some hidden structure of things was vindicated, its manifests and accountings, its wild multiform and folly. Also its taboos and limits?

As to that other, that skinny fawner, wired with voltage and vanity, that creator, his blasted face—what is to be said?

That he overstepped, that he stole fire?

Pie in the Sky

As governor of Arkansas and a candidate for president, Clinton flew home to witness the execution of lobotomized Ricky Rector. Led from his cell to the electric chair, the prisoner left the pie from his last meal in his cell, intending to eat it after his execution.

Someday somehow Ill get me
makeup of that pie
Rick shoved forkfuls of
into his soon to be
resurrected tummy
treadin, yumyumin among the
dead men walking
& hummin no doubt, and strummin
'America the beautiful.'

Why just imagine, the same
current that baked the All-
American confection
sent Rick shooting praises
altitudinous, the pie
like unto him combusted
like unto him alas
eternally
unconsumed.
Who I ask my soul
the savvy baker of this
(turned executioner—
but don't
dwell on this or that—
apples, lard, flour,
rolled out flat—

blood, bone, pore addled brain,
recipe close kept
as a sheriff's keys—
    who lo, hath wrought this wonder?

    Why pore Rick doesnt know
    his ars from a baked apple.
    Then drag him outa there for
    fifty quickened paces,
    a made-up word sufficing
urging 'Cmon Rick, quick like—
  ex-e-cu-tion, ex-ha-la-tion,
    ex-cavation'—
    then KABOOM!
    what he dont know wont hurt him.

    Sure kid cross my heart we'll
bring you right back here yer
    just desserts awaiting.

        —from *Diary of Sorts*

I Appear on a Television in Denver, Colorado, a Downer

Reader, why read on?

because this mortal body shall
put on immortality?
or because
incongruity lurks,
motley in bells, a fool?

—comes to mind
a fountain, a public square
a Belgian town.
A little bronze boy
pissing
in a stone basin.

Summer autumn winter
no defector he, let years
take their toll, elsewhere.
Like Huck Finn
he poles time's
lazy current, makes mock—
those who merely boringly
grow up, fade fast.

The sun fuels his heart, moons
meander by, a cold caress.
Stars in orbit crown the task. Behold
an ikon of sweetness;

his little handy dandy
harmlessly
jets forth, pure, pearly,
prelapsarian, a fountain in the first
garden of all!

In the basin
trout
sputter and thrive and

strollers take delight.

Schoolboys of an age,
wicked, emulous
clot together, gleeful
draw from schoolboy pants,
theirs too—
the mocking malfeasant
conspiratorial tools wagging.

Staid matrons, moms, nurses
run and run toward—
bearing on high
like pennants, small underpants—
coo, child! come cover yourself!

To no avail.
Our boy's like the three
who sing 'praise ye'
this child
of raging metals, tried by fire.

He holds in hand
the 'logos spermaticum'
    I think he
  created the world
      the child maker of all

Little boy relieve us
      believe for us—
  all things
    are good.

    —from *Diary of Sorts*

Father and Son

The following story was told me by a dear friend, the Buddhist monk, Thich Nhat Hanh.

The father of a child, aged nine or ten, was in mourning for his deceased wife. One day, he left the boy with relatives, and went on an errand to a distant town.

Pirates were marauding the district. In the father's absence, they struck. They burned the village, killed many of the people and carried off others as hostages.

The father returned, to find his home in ashes. He went about the ruined village, distraught with grief, seeking some evidence of his son. Finally he came on the remains of what seemed to be a child.

This must be all that remained of his little boy! He gathered the remains in a precious leather purse. From that day forward, he carried the ashes and bones about on his back; whether eating, walking, sleeping, praying, voyaging, the ashes of his son were his burden.

He rebuilt his home, and lived there alone.

One night, some months after the tragedy, he was asleep in his house. It was already late at night, and a knock sounded at the door.

"Who calls me at this hour?" he cried.

"It is your son. My father, I have found you at last, came the voice."

"Go away! My son is dead!" cried the father.

"No, I am not dead! I have escaped the pirates; I have passed long months seeking you."

"Go away, go away!" cried the father.

Finally, denied welcome, the child went away into the night. And the father and son never again met.

✺

Do we prefer to carry the ashes of death, instead of hearing what we indeed hear, a voice at the door—a voice of son, sister, spouse, friend? Do we prefer death to life?

All honor to the Plowshares and so many others, who open a door barred and bolted by the spirit of death against the living. . . .

Apartment I I-L

1.

I dwell in rooms
that came together from four winds
help of a flying carpet,
Aladdin's lamp,
and 200 friends at the least.
Rooms of faces and words.
The typewriter spouts, happy as coffee fresh.
Chairs, rickety and serviceable
hold out their arms.
Ingredients, beans, barley, butter, rice
implore from shelves and cupboards—
O make of us something frivolous, original
and your soul will abide content
and sprout blossoms and apples
like a tree in a body named Eden!
Busybody pots and pans
clatter like Dutch housewives—
Fill us with music, ambrosia, nectar!
Roots at window; Let me tell
how these green children fail or multiply
panting like dogs in noon, for water
water on the tongue.

And here, I almost forgot.
the door to a dark
underground drama.
Faces walk off the walls
into my theatre of dreams, good dreams.

At dawn
the faces depart, like
mimes of the Bread and Puppet troupe,
where they made foolish sense all night
of rational mad days.
                              So I can say
truthfully; Now I see
and kiss my hand to those I love
who put on once more
on a wall of no wailing
their set expression, ikons and ancestors;
Thank you, now I see.

2.

These are the rooms I go from.
An angel commands it; Go from here.
I go
to break the bones of death, to crack
the code of havocking dreams. I go from here
to judgment, to judges
by Rouault, Daumier, Goya,
their hammer crack of doom.
I go. Then, I'm told
by a guardian angel of the rooms I'm told—
When you go from here
faces of those you love
turn to the wall, and weep.
I have an angel's word.

And when I return
older, sad at times, so little of death undone
despite all sacrifice and rage
Lo, something savory, exotic
steams in a pot, the table fitly laid.

And the typewriter's iron mask
melts in a smile, and the keys
like a lover's hands
compose a love letter;
Welcome. Believe. Endure.

—from *Diary of Sorts*

Getting Old

I saw priests
like wintry wigs
or raveled birds' nests—

In despair, in youth
I longed for the day
I'd simmer down
old wine in an old bag
insipid, tractable
a necrophiliac
toward the tunnel's end.

Your gut was god
you were exemplary in the crotch
(which in marxist morphology
withered away
in the blossoming kingdom
—hyacinth, wisteria—
no Eve at the trellis rising
no moon, madness, mouth)

All a lie!
the fiery grow old fiery,
naked as a whipstock.
The sun huffs like an adder
burn baby burn
everything burns
sanity, eyeballs;
middle age is cursing God

antistrophe
to that sublime dawn bird
that sang its preincarnate
maidenhood, murder.

Now I remember.

And
if I dance
algebraic as an angel
it is
because You are
intricate motive
staggering burden—
old Father I heft and shoulder
out of the burning city.

—from *Diary of Sorts*

Less Than

The trouble was not excellence.
I carried that secret,
a laugh up my sleeve
all the public years
all the lonely years
(one and the same)
years that battered like a wind tunnel
years
like a yawn at an auction
(all the same)

Courage was not the fault
years they carried me shoulder high
years they ate me like a sandwich
(one and the same)

the fault was—dearth of courage
the bread only so-so
the beer near beer

I kept the secret under my shirt
like a fox's lively tooth, called
self knowledge.

That way
the fox eats me
before I rot.

That way I keep measure—
neither Pascal's emanation
naked, appalled
'under the infinite starry spaces'

nor a stumblebum
havocking
in Alice's doll house.

Never the less!
Summon
courage, excellence!

The two, I reflect, could
snatch us from ruin.

A fairly modest urging—
Don't kill, whatever pretext.
Leave the world unbefouled.
Don't hoard.
Stand somewhere.

And up to this hour
(Don't tell a soul)
here I am.

—from *Diary of Sorts*

Beyond

What lies beyond—
Beyond scope and skill,
beyond
wayward winds, capricious minds,
beyond, beyond despair—

lies within, plenary and pure—
compassion's clear eyed child.

What lies beyond,
beyond
dole and bribe and
browbeating eyes,
beyond mandated terror—
lies, within;
                I mean
solace, end time
sweetly present
in sad or gladsome hours—
creator Spirit, hand in mine,
a ringaround, pure light.

What lies beyond,
(diaphanous, denied,
beyond
              the death of promise)—
lies within.

Hear it;
the golden tongued
choral ode of the unborn.

—from Beyond

Afterword

Many of us know Father Daniel Berrigan and his brother Philip, who died in 2002, for their dramatic and persistent political actions in defense of the poor and disadvantaged, and particularly for their resistance to and protest of war, both conventional and nuclear. The Berrigans' stand is that the killing of a human being is never justified by any principle or belief, and that property and materiel utilized in killing has no right to exist.

Few of us know, however, that Daniel Berrigan is a prize-winning poet, or that he has been a prolific interpreter of the bible, with many books, particularly about the Hebrew prophets, to his credit. Those unacquainted with this other side of the public activist will be surprised by the texture of his writing and its honest glimpses into his heart and mind. Is Berrigan a saint, or, as others claim, morally flawed at best? Is he following the will of God as he sees it whatever the personal cost? No matter what your views on Daniel Berrigan, this book is an eye opener.

As a poet, Berrigan is personal and accessible, taking us back to a difficult childhood in an uncompromising Irish Catholic home and then carrying us through his development as he reacts to and acts out against injustice and cruelty carried out on behalf of Americans by its traditionally heroic, but misguided, government— with the tacit approval of his beloved church.

Berrigan's fables, on the other hand, express his frustration at the hypocrisy and outright stupidity of the world. For example, in "The Skinless Folk and the Elbows & Knives Folk," the world is divided into two major groups: (1) The Skinless Folk, which probably includes me and many readers of this book. We are aware and perplexed by the evils of the world and yet we demonstrate "indifference to the prospering or withering of the world Vine, or the people perilously and fruitfully appended." (2) The Elbows & Knives Folk "are a people of voracious interest in the world and its goods, services, markets, incomes, investments, politics, potential. And all, alas, for no commendable reason: for possession and control, a condition diagnosed here and there as a disease, and rightly."

The storyteller asks himself: "Does there exist a third way? He longs to believe it is so. . . . The storyteller is perhaps pointing, not to a failure of nerve, but to something deeper, more ruinous: a failure of moral imagination . . . He is haunted by the blown skin, the hapless and naked, as by a knife lodged in a stopped heart."

This is amazing stuff and well worth unraveling; though, like the questions he asks, neither light nor easy.

I approached this book with a highly primed curiosity. In many ways, I identify with the Berrigans, having experienced a variation on their upbringing. Though I may have felt as sickened by the bombs and the napalm of Vietnam as Daniel, Philip, and their accomplices, I lacked the conviction and the courage to act against the authorities who insisted a military solution was the only way to save the world from the domino effect of Communism, and who told us that the resulting deaths were unfortunate but necessary. As a Canadian it was possible to see this as an American problem having little to do with us. But while Canada was not directly involved, Canadian businesses nonetheless benefited from the war.

I recall my university years as being largely a time of frustration and confusion. It was then, through television and the other media, that we learned of the actions of Daniel and Philip Berrigan, two Catholics just like us, brought up in traditional homes, taught to be respectful and obedient, standing up to the bishops and the generals and daring to break the law in order to stop the killing of innocent civilians. They were priests just like the Redemptorists of my Holy Redeemer Parish and they were willing to go to jail for their convictions. How did they ever find the courage to do such a thing?

As a descendent, on both sides, of devout Highland Scots exiles who fled the brutal regimes of their homeland and settled on Prince Edward Island around 1774, here our family remains after more than two centuries. In our new land we lived peaceful and prosperous lives influenced by the laws of church and country. I don't recall anyone in my family protesting a decision of the government other than at the polls on Election Day. I am no longer a practicing Roman Catholic; yet, much of what I learned as a Catholic child still governs my moral sense and many of the decisions I make. This heritage may explain why I am so impressed with the courage and the sacrifices made by Daniel and his brother.

According to Murray Polner and Jim O'Grady in *Disarmed and Dangerous: The Radical Lives and Times of Daniel and Philip Berrigan,* Dan's paternal grandfather left Ireland following the Potato Famine of 1845–49 and landed in Charlottetown, the capital of Prince Edward Island, before making his way on foot to New York State. There he married and established a line of staunch Roman Catholics who were proud of their heritage and ferociously devoted to their God, their church, and their new country. While Daniel was at seminary, all of his brothers served in the military, including Philip, who received a battlefield commission, and only later became an ordained priest. Daniel's father wanted his children to be strong and manly and he did everything in his power to toughen them up. The boy Daniel was frail and meek and frequently scorned by his father; he felt himself to be an ". . . undersized myopic tacker."

I can imagine how things were at home for the sensitive Daniel. The Catholicism of my youth was two decades newer than what influenced the Berrigan home; but even so we were required to constantly examine our consciences, with our personal salvation the expressed goal.

Since his ordination in 1955, Berrigan has been faithful to his vows as a priest. Even though he hated his church's lack of leadership in opposing the Vietnam War and other injustices, he remains a loyal Catholic who loves his Jesuit Order and his church.

Berrigan needed coaxing at the beginning of his activist life. His commitment meant acceptance of the personal cost and the difficulties brought upon his family. If he and his brother would be the first of their family ever in jail, this was preferable to inaction, to doing nothing to prevent the ongoing slaughter.

A Sunday in Hell has proved to be wonderful reading and an enriching experience, presenting provocative and informative insights into the mind of Daniel Berrigan and his life of sacrifice and commitment. It saddens me that killing and murder still remain the preferred solution to conflicts among human beings. Violence against general populations has never worked in the long term and it never will. Like Berrigan, we must put on the skin of non-violent resistance and never give up the struggle.

Hugh MacDonald
Brudenell, P.E.I., August 2005

About the Authors

Daniel Berrigan is a Jesuit priest, poet, and peacemaker who has been nominated many times for the Nobel Peace Prize. He has written more than fifty books, including *The Trial of the Catonsville Nine*, And the *Risen Bread: Selected Poems 1957-1997, Testimony: The Word Made Fresh*, and *To Dwell in Peace: An Autobiography*. A member of the Catonsville Nine and Plowshares Eight, Daniel Berrigan continues to demonstrate against war and nuclear weapons and give lectures across the country about the scriptures and the call to peacemaking. He lives in New York City.

Hugh MacDonald (Afterword) has published numerous books of poetry, fiction, literary anthologies, and an award-winning children's book. He taught high school for thirty-one years before retiring to write full time. He has six children, two of whom still live with him and his wife, Sandra, in Brudenell, PEI, Canada.

A NOTE ON THE TYPE

This book was set in 11.5 point Minion with a leading of 15 points space. Minion is a 1990 Adobe Originals typeface by Robert Slimbach. Minion is inspired by classical, old style typefaces of the late Renaissance, a period of elegant, beautiful, and highly readable type designs. Created primarily for text setting, Minion combines aesthetic and functional qualities that make it highly readable.

The display font, Centaur, originally designed by Bruce Rogers for the Metropolitan Museum of Art in 1914, was released by Monotype in 1929. Modeled on letters cut by the fifteenth-century printer Nicolas Jenson, Centaur has a beauty of line and proportion that has been widely acclaimed since its release.

Composed by Jean Carbain
New York, New York

Printed and bound in the U.S.A.